DEATH, I SAID

A Charlie Chan Mystery

John L. Swann

Nicholas K. Burns Publishing
Utica, New York 13501

Nicholas K. Burns Publishing
130 Proctor Boulevard
Utica, New York 13501
www.nkbpublishing.com
nickburns@nkbpublishing.com

Copyright © 2023 John L. Swann

All rights reserved. No part of this book may be reproduced or transmitted in any form or by any means, electronic or mechanical, including photocopying, recording, or by any information storage and retrieval system without written permission from the publisher, except for the inclusion of quotations in a review.

First Edition

ISBN 978-0-9755224-2-4
Library of Congress Control Number: 2023950899

The following is a work of fiction inspired by the characters created by Earl Derr Biggers. Any resemblance to actual events or persons, living or dead, is entirely coincidental. While the primary setting is the very real San Francisco of the nineteen-thirties, the unnamed university and its campus were constructed in the author's imagination.

*For my spouse and partner,
Patricia Swann, whose success
as a writer of nonfiction, and years
of encouragement, inspired this tribute
to the detective fiction of a bygone era.*

CONTENTS

I	A SERIOUS BUSINESS	1
II	"CHARLIE, I NEED YOUR HELP"	11
III	SOME KIND OF MONEY TROUBLE	21
IV	CALLING ON AN OLD FRIEND	33
V	TEA AND REMINISCENCE	43
VI	A SHARP CRY	53
VII	THE CORONER'S REPORT	65
VIII	"SO MANY QUESTIONS ALL AT ONCE"	75
IX	SILENCE IN THE STACKS	83
X	LUNCH WITH MISS WINGET	95
XI	A GRIM SCENE	107
XII	TANGLED SKEIN OF CLUES	119
XIII	ONE LAST MYSTERY SOLVED	133
XIV	NO GREATER CALAMITY	139

PREFACE

I discovered Charlie Chan through the Warner Oland and Sidney Toler films when I was 6 or 7. In those days—the middle of the last century—television stations needed something to fill the weekend hours, and black-and-white movies came in handy. So, long before their widespread availability through cable TV, the internet, etc., most of the 20th Century Fox Chan mysteries provided an escape from weekend boredom—probably for many viewers, but certainly for me.

Apart from Chan, TV's fill-the-time offerings included the Basil Rathbone-Nigel Bruce Sherlock Holmes wartime movies; during the period when I was eagerly tuning in to watch both detectives, I devoured Conan Doyle's Holmes novels and stories.

Then, I sought out the Earl Derr Biggers Chan novels available at the library. Chan in print was better, in some ways; he was different from the Hollywood version. To a young reader, as I then was, the Biggers style—dated though it seems to many, of course—was something new and exotic.

As I re-read the books years later, I came to regret that their author's early death had ended the series. Recently, it occurred to me that maybe I could apply myself to telling the next Chan story, the one that Biggers might have written.

After a few fits and starts, I decided to send Charlie to college, roping in some characters from previous Biggers books to give the new work some continuity. Maybe, I thought, the reappearance of John Quincy Winterslip, from the first novel, and Rose Chan, would appeal to readers who knew those names from the Chan canon.

Fans of the Chan films will find this work familiar, too, since I found myself constructing scenes and dialogue for a novel—decidedly uncinematic, especially by 21st-century standards—but realized that I was also drawing on Oland and Toler's performances. So, I suppose that *Death, I Said* represents elements of both forms.

Finally, I would be remiss if I did not address, briefly, the Chan character's sometimes-troubling history, since any attempt to continue the Biggers stories, without completely "correcting" the characters, language, etc., to conform to current expectations, could be offensive to some.

I have tried to make this story a genuine representation of how Biggers depicted Chan in that period, but I have also omitted the stereotypes that cropped up in some of the books and films. For a fuller treatment of why the Chan character, on the whole, deserves a positive interpretation—despite Hollywood's long-ago failures—I wholeheartedly recommend the work of Yunte Huang.

I hope that this humble work finds favor with those for whom it is intended: the devoted fans of a small but influential chapter in American mystery and detective literature, and all those who still enjoy a good Chan film.

CHAPTER I

A SERIOUS BUSINESS

The young woman jumped from the street car to the curb and ran down the street—no easy feat, given her businesslike dress and heeled shoes. She was determined to be early, not simply on time. And certainly, definitely, not late. Despite her outward appearance—the very picture of a modern, urban worker in the 1930s—both her cherished Chinese heritage and her father's frequent admonitions had instilled in her the belief that to arrive before the appointed time was the easiest way of all to show respect, especially in the current circumstances. And to be late was not just a sign of disrespect; today, it could spell disaster for her plans.

Dodging pedestrians moving at a more leisurely pace, she counted down the blocks: just one more to her destination. Her wrist-watch told her that there was still time. Slowing to a brisk walk, she approached her destination, an old brick building (*Older than me*, she thought), climbing its solid steps and struggling briefly with imposing wooden double-doors. Heart pounding, and almost out of time, she took a deep breath and let it out slowly.

Now, down the hall; past one office, then another, then another, all the way to the one at the end of the wing. Breathing almost normally, and still five minutes before her time, she confirmed the name and title painted on the door's frosted glass window.

She knocked firmly, and waited.

"But why do you want to become a lawyer?"

The dean posed this question in his best cross-examining voice, with furrowed brow punctuated by graying eyebrows. The recipient of his gaze met it sturdily, unflinchingly. Once the interview had begun, preparation and poise served her well, and the dash to arrive on time was forgotten.

"Because I have grown up with a great respect for the law and for justice, and I want to help people. Especially people accused unjustly," she added quickly. "My work here, my grades—I am qualified to study law, and, well, it is my dream."

"That may be, but you'll find there's nothing very dreamlike about *Blackstone*." The dean's frown subsided, replaced by a more welcoming expression. "And I'm happy to say that this interview is something of a formality since, as you say, your scholarly work as an undergraduate speaks well of you. And so do the faculty who refer you," he added.

"Then—?"

"It gives me great pleasure to confirm your admission, and I wish you every success." The dean shook the newly minted law student's hand and returned her portfolio.

"Thank you! Thank you, Dean Bernardo—I am so happy, I—"

"Welcome to our program. Just see Miss Winget in the provost's office about the position there. She'll take care of you."

After delivering welcome news to the young lady— *She'll go far*, he mused—the dean's mind returned to the

A SERIOUS BUSINESS

matter at hand. Charging a pipe of uncertain vintage with a malodorous blend of domestic tobacco, he put flame to bowl and sent up smoke signals of mental distress. *What, in heaven's name, was to be done?*

Leaving the austere setting of the dean's study, Rose made her way down the hall to the provost's office, presenting her portfolio to a prim woman of uncertain age who looked up from a stack of letters inquiringly.

"Miss Winget? Dean Bernardo said to see you—I'm new," Rose said, as though being new explained all things.

"I'm sure you are—new, that is," returned Gertrude Winget. "But what program?"

"Oh, my goodness! Evening law. And here is my portfolio."

She handed over the folder. Miss Winget examined it through reading glasses of surpassing strength, judging from their thickness. The secretary (a mere title, she was actually much more than that in the workings of the office) consulted a list and picked up a fountain pen.

"So, for this academic year you plan to spend your days in this office and your evenings in class? Are you sure working here won't get in the way of your studies?"

"Oh, no—I want to learn the law, of course, but I also need practical experience. And," she added shyly, "the money will help, too."

"Your first name is Rose, is that correct? And no middle name?"

"That's right, yes. My father said there were so many of us that one name for each child was enough."

"He must have a sense of humor, and I hope you take after him. You'll need one here."

"I do, I think. That is, I have a sense of humor," said

Rose. "But why? I thought studying law was a serious business."

Miss Winget paused from adding Rose's name to the office staff list.

"That it is, for some students. But we have very few young women here. The practice of law," she observed tartly, "is a man's world, and I'm afraid you'll find many of the men here would just as soon keep it that way. But don't you fret—any of them gives you trouble, you come to me. I'll soon set them straight."

"Why, thank you, but we've only just met, and—"

"Doesn't matter. Sized you up right away. And anyway, I make it my business to look out for the few young women here," Winget concluded firmly. "Are you a native of San Francisco?"

"No, but I'm beginning to feel like I belong here after four years of college. I am from Hawaii—my family is still there, but I came here to go to school. I love the city."

There was a momentary silence as Miss Winget scanned Rose's curriculum vitae, and closed the folder.

"Thank you for your help! Do you need any other information from me?"

Miss Winget paused, a look of uncertainty crossing her face briefly. "Hmm? No, my dear, everything I need is here in the material you shared with the dean. Do you have any questions for me, anything I can help you with?"

Rose smiled and extended her hand.

"No, no; thank you. You've been very kind—both you and the dean. When shall I start work?"

Gertrude Winget shook the proffered hand and returned the smile.

"Monday morning, and the office opens at eight, sharp. I'll see you then—mind you, be here on time. The new fall term means a fair amount of work for this office, and I'm glad you're going to be here to help out."

Rose turned and left, feeling nearly giddy at the thought of the coming week—a new job, and her first class as a student of the law. She would be over the moon all weekend long.

The president reveled in his title. It was still so new that references to "the president" in a faculty meeting, such as this especially tedious one, still surprised him, if but for a moment, when others nodded in his direction. For Christopher Emerson had come of age in this college, now a university, beginning as an undergraduate so many years ago, somehow making his way from a bachelor's degree to a faculty appointment. Years of toil had yielded not only tenure, but the first of what became an increasing number of administrative tasks and appointments, interrupted only by his obtaining further academic credentials back east. He became a full professor, served as dean. Then provost. Finally, in fulfillment of his long-simmering ambition, he had ascended to the summit. He was not simply "Dr. Emerson," or "Christopher Emerson, Ph.D., D.Litt." He was, in fact, "President Emerson."

Apart from the years spent solidifying his academic credentials in Philadelphia, he was a fixture here. And that was his dream: to have stayed, risen to the heights and remained. In his mind, he saw his entire future presidency laid out in roseate terms: Son of San Francisco, twentieth-century academic visionary, longest-serving president in the university's history. He foresaw a far-off day when his large-as-life portrait would be unveiled in the Academic Hall, affirming a legacy unsurpassed, unequaled by any academic leader in the state.

True, his view from the summit was not all sweetness and light. Approaching the end of his first academic year as president, he had already seen a fair amount of conflict between and among members of the faculty. And he had, he thought, done well in his chief internal leadership duties. *Too bad about Merriweather,* he thought. *Poor chap took it hard at first, but he seems to have come round. Fine academic, but definitely not presidential material. Old Gordon will do well as provost for the duration.*

The provost's mind wandered. *Good heavens,* he thought. *Will this fellow never come to the point?* The meeting was one of many the provost dreaded every week, and it felt like a Dante circle (one of the lower ones) in his career perdition.

All his adult life, Gordon Merriweather had aspired to be the president of a university, any university, and his early advancement leading to the number two job, academic provost, was encouraging.

Until now.

Passed over by the university's governing board in the most recent presidential search for a younger man, a hated rival, Merriweather had alternated this past year between anger, despair and resignation. These shifting emotions went unobserved by his colleagues because the provost (*for life, probably,* he brooded) was a master of the neutral expression; countless faculty committee meetings had taught him to keep any and all reactions to matters at hand under wraps.

Despite his serene expression, Merriweather's mind was aflame with indignation—rage, even—and the beginnings of a strategy that, he had begun to realize, might be the only course left to him.

***

Dean Bernardo, whose academic career was nearing its distinguished end, was troubled. He relit his pipe for a third time and reviewed the somewhat disordered contents of a complicated mind. All year long he had tried to ignore a situation that only seemed to grow worse. But what to do? He had little evidence, and certainly no proof. Mostly just hints, allegations and a growing sense of unease; but his instincts seldom failed him in more mundane matters, so he was increasingly convinced that there was, indeed, fire as well as smoke.

The junior faculty—even some attending this pestilential meeting—amused themselves by comparing Dean Aloysius Bernardo, Ph.D., M.A., etc., etc., to the film actor C. Aubrey Smith. Admittedly, the resemblance was uncanny—the brow dominated by bushy, gray eyebrows; steely (but at times, kindly) eyes; a weary, Hungarian mustache; the square jaw. The dean could've been the actor's brother. Even his clipped manner of speaking, and a Boston-Brahmin-meets-Oxford-don accent, suggested a stage professor. Blissfully unaware of the affectionate comparison, the dean was, in fact, a bit past his intellectual prime. His absentmindedness was growing, and he had been known to nod off during lengthy afternoon meetings.

This situation now, he thought, *what a muddle! What am I to do?* Clearly something untoward was afoot, and he could see no way to avoid—at minimum—a financial morass that could mar his career with a dreadful blot. Damaging not only to him, but to the university he had served so well for so many years. The effect on the institution—the students, the faculty—that was what concerned him most. He sent another smoky plume to join others rising toward the oak-paneled ceiling.

This blasted fiscal maelstrom, what on earth was the

radix causa? (The dean's thoughts, like his lengthier utterances, frequently lapsed into Latin whether or not the occasion called for it.) *Not a whirlpool, perhaps,* he amended, *but there must be a root cause, some reason behind it all. Where has the money gone? And who is responsible?*

Some of his colleagues thought Professor Gilberto "Gilvie" Silva a radical; others dismissed him as an idiot. In the suspicious atmosphere of the 'thirties, his Portuguese origins—unkind students sometimes referred to him incorrectly as "a Spanish nut"—led some to suspect his politics. Surely he was a leftist, they whispered. San Francisco's melting pot was not much noticed in the halls of the university, where faculty still wore academic robes throughout the day, and sometimes it seemed more like the nineteenth century than the twentieth. Professor Silva and his imperfect English—his accent was decidedly Iberian—stood out in the ranks of the nearly all-white, mostly male faculty.

And his outsider status rankled.

A sociologist, Silva tended to see his personal and professional situation through the lens of his studies (and a tendency toward pessimism). His thoughts teemed with an all-inclusive condemnation of fools and foolish things. First, the world was chaos. Second, governments—especially the American government—were, at best, inept; at worst, corrupt and intentionally malevolent. Third—and most aggravating to him professionally—people were fools; the whole university administration, his colleagues, the students. Although, he conceded, the students were capable of some degree of intellectual redemption—they were still young; they could be taught, perhaps. They were just *dorminhocos,* sleepyheads.

Silva reserved his angriest thoughts for the president and provost—the dean he dismissed as *avelho tolo*, an old fool—but Emerson and Merriweather, they were incompetent, corrupt. And they had insulted him—they should be removed.

His anger had begun to take a potentially sinister turn.

The man relaxed in the cool of the evening—welcome breezes ruffling the pages of a newspaper on his lap. The news of the day was of little concern; he knew before buying the paper that his recent work had found no place there.

Charlie Chan sighed.

As one who had spent much of his life in the peculiar gap between East and West, he struggled to maintain the equanimity of character that, he firmly believed, his ancestors had possessed. Had he not been reared to respect them, and to observe the rites? And to follow the ancient wisdom, the precepts of the ancients? Yet his professional endeavors, all his striving—it left him, at times, at odds with philosophies of humility, modesty and the like.

Perhaps it was enough, now, after opportunities and success that chance had placed in his path, for him to be content with the humdrum of policing in a quiet setting. Petty thievery, small-time criminals—these were his to address now, and it was important to preserve the peace, even in a sleepy tropical town. Still, at times he felt keenly that his talents were wasted here.

"Here" was paradise for more and more mainland visitors these days; "tourism" had become a chamber of commerce byword. From his lanai looking down on Punchbowl Hill, he chided himself for a moment. So many came so far just to experience for a few weeks the beauty of these islands that he was taking for granted. And what man could be unhappy in life with a family such as his? Devoted wife, eleven children, a house filled with laughter—and, at times, a few tears, of course. A middle-aged man (some would say he was in the prime of life), he could look forward to observing and celebrating the next generation's many successes, even though they were, and would become, more "Americanized" than he.

Even now, his older children were pursuing success as young adults. The oldest boy had stayed close to home, plying the trade of bank clerk and remaining a part of the family circle, a daily example for the younger children. And his eldest daughter remained far away, continuing her studies in pursuit of a career on the mainland. He was simultaneously proud of her accomplishments—and troubled by her absence; should not the eldest daughter honor tradition as well as ambition? (And, Chan reflected wryly, a grandchild or two would be welcome as well!)

The letter received today had come none too soon, almost as though the fates had discerned his thoughts of his yearning for a new professional challenge. This proposed case was not as complex as those that had brought him past satisfactions (and some publicity, too), but what need had he of a seemingly unsolvable case or further acclaim? His correspondent's request provided an opportunity for not only an investigative puzzle, but also a change of scenery—and a chance to visit and reconnect with family.

He recalled the words of the ancient sage, "When the times are quiet, it is easy to act." Professionally speaking, "quiet" was an understatement. His chief could spare him. At home, Henry—the eldest—would help Chan's wife maintain the workings of a very active household.

A trip to the mainland would require preparation, and Chan was already looking forward to the voyage.

CHAPTER II

"CHARLIE, I NEED YOUR HELP"

Dear Charlie,

I hope that you and your entire family are well, and that you have not forgotten the naïve young man who attempted to act as your junior assistant several years ago. My youthful adventure with you on the islands (I feel I can write "youthful" without exaggeration—I am, after all, a wise old man of more than 30!) was a turning point for me, as you know, and I think fondly of you, and those few weeks of excitement, often. I'm sure Aunt Minerva, if she knew of this letter, would want me to extend her very best wishes to you and yours. Now, to business—for I am, now, a man of business!

Charlie, I need your help.

Chan's expression remained unchanged as he absorbed the rest of the letter. John Quincy's "junior assistant" experience had come about after the murder of his Winterslip cousin Dan, a longtime Honolulu resident. After the case was solved, John Quincy had found professional opportunity with another family member, Roger Winterslip, a well-known San Francisco engineer and builder.

His plea for help stemmed from an assignment he had received to examine a local university's finances—

confidentially—at the request of its board; specifically, from Roger, who served on the board. What he had found so far, John Quincy wrote, suggested the need for a real investigator, not just a financial expert.

Having just come to the conclusion that I was in over my head, and not knowing where to turn for help with a sensitive matter such as this, the mention of your name by my cousin Roger prompted me to write to you. (He also mentioned that one of your offspring is a student here?)

Chan smiled. Rose, the oldest of his daughters, was dear to him; he was happy that she was making her own way. Always she had been independent, but she had been gone since last summer; it was now almost May. He felt her absence keenly.

I'm hoping, Charlie, that you can combine a family visit with a little unofficial detective work. My firm would pay you as a consultant and cover all your expenses, and I would be pleased to offer you all the hospitality that a rising pillar of the community has at his command!

Before I close, please know that your kindness to me as I struggled with the loss of Carlota will never be forgotten. I have slowly come to terms with that short chapter of my life, in which happiness was followed so quickly by bereavement.

My best to your wife and family, and I hope to hear from you soon.

Sincerely,

John Quincy Winterslip

Chan refolded the letter and considered. It would be pleasant to see Rose for the first time since her departure for law school many months ago, and his chief would, no doubt, approve a vacation, even a leave of absence. His duties of late had been unchallenging at best. Perhaps young Winterslip's problem would present a refreshing change, a new puzzle to solve.

His mind made up, Charlie Chan set matters in motion.

In the decades since the 1906 earthquake and fire, San Francisco had recovered remarkably well. Oldtimers might lament a loss of gritty character and unique culture, but no one under a certain age seemed to regret what had happened since the devastation left its mark. By most accounts, it was still a wide-open town in many ways, even though much of its roguish past—dark doings on the waterfront—had receded into history and lore. Prohibition came and went, and the continued simmering of the East-West melting pot showed no signs of cooling. San Francisco was an increasingly vibrant city that mixed past, present and future.

Despite the effects of the national, even global, financial crisis of the current decade, the city was holding its own—and better. After several bitter years, people seemed to be breathing new life into public spaces; commercial activity of all kinds had gradually flourished anew. And, most visible of all, two great bridges were well on their way to completion, providing a great many jobs, of course, but also visibly manifesting progress—and a brilliant future.

Whatever befell the city overall, it had retained its essential identity—it continued to exemplify a city by a bay, where the waterfront was both point of arrival and place of departure. Passengers, shipping, people with commercial interests, those seeking employment, the curious—these and more contributed to the ebb and flow of traffic and tumult. To a first-time visitor, the Embarcadero and vicinity presented a kind of bedlam, a seething of human activity—part disturbed anthill, part controlled chaos. Starting well before dawn, the district came to life with a trickle of commercial traffic that each day grew into a stream of loading, unloading, buying, selling, trading, transferring—a world market in a single neighborhood. The scent of roasting coffee hung over parts of the district, since incoming shipments of beans lately plucked from faraway trees were a constant source of the freshest possible brew imaginable. In addition to the locals, merchants and workers from all over the world constituted a veritable League of Nations, and a dozen or more native tongues mingled with the shouts of delighted children competing for pieces of fruit fresh off the boat.

Matson liners had come and gone for years, and Charlie Chan—while not a frequent traveler—was no stranger to the rituals of arrival. He joined other passengers from the *Lurline* pouring onto the docks, where a welcoming crowd waited. Scanning the eager faces, he quickly spotted Rose and made his way through the throng.

"Dad!" she cried, as they exchanged a warm embrace. "Just look at you—the picture of health. Welcome to San Francisco!"

"My heart fills with gladness at this moment of reunion," Chan returned tenderly. "I bring you greetings from your mother, and your brothers and sisters. They send combined love of entire family.

"But you," he continued with a twinkle, "less than a year ago a girl departed from home, and now I see the fashion of a young professional woman. Perhaps you have . . . business appointment?"

"Same old detective dad," Rose laughed. "But I'm not dressed up for any reason more mysterious than welcoming my celebrity father to California in style. How was the crossing? Smooth as last time?"

"I enjoyed typical trip of man who strives to avoid ocean voyages," her father said, smiling. "And my discomfort was not as great as my eager anticipation of our reunion."

As they talked, the crowd thinned. A well-dressed man in his early thirties approached. Although his hat dipped low over his eyes, Chan thought he was familiar—an expected visitor from the past.

"Charlie Chan!" cried John Quincy Winterslip—for it was, indeed, Chan's one-time investigative amanuensis. "It's hard to believe you're really here. I am so glad; I hardly know how to thank you, I just—"

"Begging your pardon, but it is not yet time for thanks since I have done nothing so far but arrive," Chan pointed out. "Your kind words overwhelm me, and please permit me to perform social duty without further delay. This young lady is my daughter Rose."

"Oh! I've already made the acquaintance of Ro— of Miss Chan," Winterslip said hastily. "My recent visits to the university—some of them have involved time in the provost's office where she holds forth. Rumor has it she'll be in charge of the whole show soon."

Rose laughed. "Don't pay any attention to him, dad. He razzes everyone he meets on campus, and probably everyone he encounters in the city, too."

"I recall a young man some years ago with very similar personality who provided able assistance to me during a difficult investigation," Chan replied. "In fact, that young man has grown into this pillar of San Francisco business community. But please, enlighten me: What is the precise meaning of 'razzes'?"

"Dad, you have eleven kids! You still aren't fluent in American slang?" Rose raised an eyebrow in mock surprise. "I must say, though, that your formal English is really becoming—well, more formal. The classes you wrote me about—how are they? You must be an A student."

Chan acknowledged the compliment with a slight bow. "Every good daughter honors her father with suitable flattery," he said. "But I can return the favor by pointing out that your university studies inspired me to advance my understanding of this most complex English language, even American-style.

"I have, so far, pursued both grammar and conversational English in two classes, and also I continue to study the philosophers of ancient East. And the less-ancient West." Chan grimaced and continued in mock disgust. "Philosophy of both teaches patience, a quality much needed as I continue to explore English grammar—how can such a young language have more rules than Chinese?— with its articles, prepositions, tenses . . . and always, always exceptions to its many rules. I make—I *have made*—some progress but I foresee long road ahead. As an old Chinese saying puts it, man must both *live* till he is old—and *learn* till he is old."

Rose and Winterslip laughed at Chan's linguistic analysis.

"Well, your progress shows," Rose said proudly. "You'll fit right in at the university—you'll hear a lot of high-toned talk there."

"Say, I hate to break up this joyful reunion, but can I offer my services as chauffeur to our distinguished visitor and his charming daughter?" said Winterslip. "My car is nearby, and the time for a midday meal approacheth. All this educational talk is making me hungry. What say the two of you to a bite of San Francisco's finest cuisine?"

The suggestion was an agreeable one. Having collected Chan's humble luggage, the trio departed for Winterslip's roadster. With the auto's top down in celebration of the fine weather, the trio sped off in search of a suitable luncheon spot.

With typical weekend crowds and their vehicles to navigate, Winterslip proved himself a capable driver. He and Rose made conversation, and Chan's thoughts turned to the young man's misfortune. His prospects were bright when they had parted in Honolulu a decade ago: a young bride from the islands, a promising career awaiting him on the mainland. Sadly, the newlywed couple's happiness was short-lived. Chan's condolences upon learning of Winterslip's bereavement had seemed inadequate, somehow, to the detective. But the newly widowed youth had responded stoically, writing Chan that he was grateful for the happiness he and his beloved Carlota had shared, however brief.

The screech of the car's brakes brought Chan back to the present. "Here we are, and I'm famished—quite hollow, in fact," Winterslip announced happily. "Lady and gentleman, I bid you welcome to John's Grill and Oyster Parlor. And not *my* grill," he added. "Our shared given name is just a happy coincidence."

The three did full justice to a lunch of fried oysters and Saratoga chips, topped off by baked apples with cream, before discussing the matter at hand. "The problem," said Winterslip, as they lingered over coffee, "concerns certain matters that have come to the attention of the dean, who unburdened himself to my cousin Roger—you may recall I'm attached to his firm?—and it was agreed that I would poke around a bit, in a completely confidential manner.

"In fact," he continued, "you and I should continue this conversation later on, perhaps, that is—"

"Oh, sure," Rose interjected. "You men go off and solve all the problems. Why include a mere slip of a girl who might, just might, be able to help!"

"Female point of view always welcome, as far as I am concerned," said her father placidly. "But this young man is pursuing inquiries with a guarantee of confidentiality, and we must respect his commitment to maintaining same. However," he continued, "confidentiality does not prevent you from keeping open eyes and ears."

Rose smiled broadly. "Thanks, Dad! You can be sure I'll do just that."

With luncheon concluded, Rose took her leave— "I have errands," she announced—and Winterslip offered to give Chan a driving tour of the city and its recent developments, en route to his hotel.

The sightseeing was brief but covered a wide sweep of the city's high points, some that Chan observed were little changed since his last visit. Others—especially the two signature bridge projects underway—Winterslip pointed out with the pride of a convert. Despite his Boston upbringing, he had passed through the "wandering Winterslip" stage of life early on, and now considered San Francisco "his" city.

"This concludes our tour, please tip generously," quipped the younger man, as he guided the roadster toward Chan's hotel, through busy streets awash in motorists and pedestrians. "And now, to business."

"Your most recent letter described money troubles

at the university," Chan recalled. "But details were few. I suggest you start from best place of all in tale-telling: the beginning."

"Where to start, where to start," Winterslip murmured. "I suppose my part in this drama begins with my cousin Roger; he's the reason I'm here at all, as you know. He serves on the university board—I think I mentioned that in my letter.

"Roger received a hush-hush appeal from the dean—one Aloysius Bernardo. I've spoken to him; he's an elderly fellow—been at the university for donkey's years—and is, generally, reliable. A bit dithery, but sound. I think he's where you should start."

Chan was silent for a moment. Winterslip navigated to a spot on the street around the corner from the detective's hotel and turned off the engine. Chan appeared lost in thought for several seconds; to Winterslip, it seemed much longer.

"All persons desire riches, perhaps, but it has also been written that 'he who speaks does not know.' Understandable that this Bernardo may have voiced concerns about money troubles even though he does not, himself, have full and complete information. He suspects, perhaps, but he does not know who are the guilty ones. I understand from your letter's description that some money goes missing from the university, and that it has happened more than once—maybe even frequently? And he has not taken his concerns elsewhere because he does not know, or because he fears a scandal?"

"And that's where I, where we, come in," said Winterslip. "Roger can't get involved directly because he's a trustee, a board member. You may think, as I do, that a board member would be the perfect person to poke around a bit. I put this to Roger, but he was adamant. He wants to stay above the fray, to avoid, as he put it, even the appearance of meddling. Hence his direction to me, and my appeal to you. Above all, he wants us to exercise discretion. We can talk to old Bernardo to start—I've already made an initial overture. I've generally been spending a little time on the campus as a kind of community do-gooder, so that my presence doesn't arouse suspicion. And you can play the dutiful parent—visit Rose, meet her bosses, tour the campus."

Chan smiled. Exiting the vehicle, he grasped his single suitcase in one hand and lifted the other in a farewell gesture. "I suggest we proceed cautiously; parental visit will do for a start, but well-educated folk who work at college not all lacking in common sense—and suspicion. The presence of a middle-aged Chinese will not go unnoticed. Maybe once introductions happen, certain persons can be invited to meet later—perhaps at Winterslip offices?"

"Certainly. Whatever you say, Charlie. Roger would have liked to meet you, but he's out of town. So on his behalf, thank you for taking on," Winterslip said, with a perplexed look, "whatever it is, exactly, that we'll be taking on."

CHAPTER III
SOME KIND OF MONEY TROUBLE

Chan awoke early, immediately aware of the faint sounds of other hotel guests, and staff. The city's humming, thrumming background noise—even at this early hour—reminded him that Honolulu was far away. His thoughts turned to family still slumbering there and what their day would bring. As the children grew older, he felt even occasional absences from home deeply. This visit, he resolved, would be as brief as possible, although it was a joy to see Rose in the first blush of professional success.

Breaking his fast with tea and toasted sourdough bread in the hotel dining room, Chan consulted a traveler's map. The university was several blocks distant, and he relished the chance to see some of the city up-close. Yesterday's brief motor tour had reminded him that San Francisco's evolution continued, with things seen in previous visits replaced by the impact of economic hardship and the beginnings of recovery from it.

San Francisco was several cities in one: the old and new; the coarse and refined; rich, poor, American, foreign; the young and impertinent jostling the old and staid. Pockets of racial and ethnic diversity dotted the urban area; in the main it represented a marriage of the transplanted Atlantic West and the Pacific East. The cacophony of activity in the city's busier districts, such as the clatter and clang of streetcar systems on Market Street, was balanced by quieter neighborhoods steeped in a less frantic sensibility. And, as the recent maritime workers walkout and the general strike that followed had reminded everyone—as if they had forgotten!— the city had planted itself next to the ocean and had blossomed therefrom.

On this trip, no matter how brief, Chan planned to pay his respects to family—a cousin, Chan Kee Lim, had lived for many years in Chinatown—and that duty was more welcome, now that Rose was a boarder in his cousin's Waverly Street residence. The detective's previous visits to his more conservative cousin had been marked by Chan Kee Lim's ill-concealed disapproval of Charlie's "Westernness," his profession, and the other indications that he was, after many years, more American than Chinese. But this time, Chan was curious to see if his cousin—whose devotion to the old ways he deeply respected, even when family friction occurred—had mellowed at all, now that he was master of a household with "two Roses."

For each man had a daughter with that very Western-sounding name, and the cousins were about the same age. And both daughters were very much more Western even than Charlie Chan. While his Rose pursued her studies, cousin Rose (Kee Lim called her Li Mei, "Pretty Rose") was an operator in the Chinatown telephone exchange, and a night-school business student. Perhaps, Chan thought, Kee Lim had moderated his views about old and new worlds, as other members of the extended family continued to explore the twentieth century's opportunities. All except Kee Lim's wife, Chan So, of course; she remained devoted; first, to her husband; second, to her children; and third, to the ancient ways that Kee Lim had impressed on

SOME KIND OF MONEY TROUBLE

her from their first meeting many years ago.

Approaching his destination, Chan sighed and put aside thoughts of family. Chinatown would have to wait, as he had other matters on hand. From several visits to San Francisco, he knew something of the city's history, its many neighborhoods, its high (and low) society. But until today, he had not become acquainted with another of its distinct communities: the academic world.

Some visitors to any university campus have drawn comparisons, favorable or not, to cloistered monasteries. And the words "academic world" can connote an existence well apart from the so-called "real world" and its common herd. Chan would find that his destination was very much separate from the city that surrounded it.

The university was a mix of older buildings—some dating to its founding several decades ago—and newer additions. The academic administrators held forth in one of the more seasoned brick structures, a four-story block that sported enough ivy on the outside and general must-iness on the inside to provide the proper atmosphere of distinguished learning and intellectual prowess. The office Chan sought was on the second floor, and he presented himself to the gatekeeper.

"Good morning to you. I am seeking Miss Chan, please? Is she available?"

"Well, good morning, I'm Miss Winget. You must be the father—heard you would be visiting," Gertrude Winget replied crisply. "Miss Chan is in a meeting with the provost and a few others. Please have a seat. She'll be out soon."

Winget's words were punctuated by raised voices, the opening and slamming of a door and the appearance of an agitated man. He glared at Miss Winget, ignored Chan, and stormed out of the office, leaving a trail of muttered multilingual profanity in his wake.

"Humph!" Winget dismissed the brief tempest. "You'll pardon any dramatics you encounter here, I hope. Our faculty are truly wonderful—for the most part."

Chan smiled. "It is said that every family has its own issues—even the university family."

Winget's rejoinder was interrupted by a small stream of academics, apparently emerging from the same gathering that their angry colleague had departed a moment before. Last in the parade was Rose Chan.

"Dad! Have you been here long?"

"Long enough to meet Miss Winget and experience your colleague thundering through office—in search of happiness elsewhere, perhaps?"

Miss Winget barely concealed a smile as Rose said with a laugh, "Oh, you mean Professor Silva! Yes, he was not pleased with—well, many things. Too many," she continued, "to go into now. Especially since it's time for your tour of the university!"

Chan nodded. "I am in your capable hands." He turned to Winget. "So pleased to have met you, and I offer you my very best wishes for success in your duties."

"Enjoy your tour," she replied, looking up from the stacks of papers on her desk. Gertrude Winget watched father and daughter depart, chatting happily, and wondered: a family visit and nothing more?

She thought not.

Down the hall from the provost's office, two grizzled men dressed for janitorial work took stock of recent events, economically sharing a single cigarette. The two also shared a last name—Poovey—thanks to the Welsh grandfather who had reared them. Caspar and

Paul Poovey were a two-man information bureau on the campus; they seemed to see, hear, know—or suspect—all things. Since their duties took them everywhere, separately and together, they were privy to snatches of conversation and bits of gossip unavailable to the university campus hoi polloi. In private, they exchanged "the latest" in their grandfather's native language. While working in the presence of others, their habitual silence was only occasionally punctuated by a pure and lilting Welsh phrase, or an excitable bilingual burst of "Welglish," which was said to be their true tongue. Students, faculty, administrators—all who knew them spoke rather more freely than cautiously in their presence, not knowing or caring how much, if anything, the two men understood.

Some long-ago university faculty wit had dubbed them "Castor and Pollux," and by these droll nicknames they were affectionately known. Hardly anyone on campus could have produced their real names.

"What's up, then? What news?" Castor, the younger, addressed his companion with the studied lack of enthusiasm they applied to even the juiciest bits of campus gossip.

"Folks hereabouts are like the lady who raised her petticoat skirts too late," Pollux replied. "Always a-worryin' 'bout the way things might've been, or could ha' been— or should've—"

"I take your meanin' well enough. What, in pair-teek-yuh-lurr, do you refer to?"

"Same as always. The money—a fair tidy sum gone, so it's said."

"And?"

Pollux returned the half-smoked cigarette and emitted a single smoke ring before replying.

"A detective—aye, 'cometh Andronicus.'" Pollux was

fond of reusing classical phrases he had overheard on his rounds.

"Away with your fancy speech—who's coming? What detective?"

"I didn't catch the name, but he's said to be good at his trade—and comes from quite a distance."

Castor grunted. "Maybe they need someone from a ways away to sort out their money troubles."

"For all their eddication, they lack the sense to shelter during a heavy rain. Otherwise, they'd tend to their own troubles."

"That's as may be—" Castor extinguished what little remained of the cigarette beneath a heel and swept it into a crack in the floor. "I'm off to t'other building. Keep yer eyes peeled and ears sharp."

Pollux nodded, and the two parted.

"I guess Mr. Winterslip is an old friend of yours," Rose asked her father as they strolled across the campus lawn. "Have you known him a long time?"

"When you were much younger, some ten years ago, you were not so much interested in parental doings, but you may recall Winterslip murder case—it was his cousin who died, and this John Quincy Winterslip was my helpful collaborator in the successful investigation."

"And now he's helping you again?"

"Say, rather, that he has asked aging detective to help him with confidential matter—and so I am provided welcome opportunity to visit oldest daughter."

They paused near an ornate fountain to let pass a small group of chattering students. Rose waited, then looked quickly at her father.

"You mean the money trouble?"

Chan's eyebrows rose.

"How does junior employee at university learn the nature of confidential matter? Is this 'money trouble' known to"—Chan gestured in the direction of the nearby students—"everyone?"

"No, no," Rose said hastily. "Not everyone! And I may be a 'junior employee,' but working in the provost's office I hear a lot of things without, well, trying to. And sometimes people think out loud or talk to themselves. It's almost as though they forget I'm there.

"I don't really *know* much of anything," she added. "Nothing specific, that is. Just that the financial situation is not what it should be, and old Dean Bernardo is very worried."

"This worry—do others share it, or does this dean bear his burden alone?"

Rose considered. "I think Miss Winget knows some-thing, or suspects something. She seems to know just about everything that goes on at the university. I mean, it's just a feeling I have. It's not that she's confided in me or anything like that."

The tour was brief compared to those offered to more typical campus visitors, but it provided the necessary pretext for a private father-daughter conversation. By now, they had returned to the main building. Rose paused outside a set of double-doors on the ground floor.

"I'm not a great tour guide, but you need to see our auditorium." She opened one of the doors, and they peered into a large room, an amphitheater of a few hundred seats facing a curtained stage. "Our main events happen here—convocation at the start of the year, and commencement at the end. Plenty of 'Pomp and Circumstance,' and lots of speeches."

"And you take part in these big events?"

"Usually just as a member of the supporting cast," Rose grinned. "You know—behind-the-scenes things that need to happen so the VIPs on the stage can make those long speeches. If your visit lasts long enough, spring commencement is only a week away, and I can get you a front-row seat."

"Happily that circumstance will not arise. As much as I am enjoying this academic experience, I hope to conclude my business soon and return to your mother and brothers and sisters."

"Aw, dad! You just got here, and you're ready to leave?" Charlie Chan sighed.

"The happy man stays at home, not even going out of his door, and knows of all things. Maybe someday I will be that happy man. Still," he continued, "plenty pleased to see you—if only for a few days."

"Your humble daughter is likewise pleased to see the best dad in this hemisphere," Rose said affectionately. "I know being away from home isn't your favorite thing, but I'm glad you were able to come visit. Let's make the most of it!"

Father and daughter parted at the door to the provost's office; Rose was unaware that Chan was headed for a meeting with the dean and John Quincy Winterslip, away from the inquiring eyes and minds of the academic community.

"Dean Aloysius Bernardo, meet Inspector Charlie Chan."

Winterslip had brought the academic and the detective together in his office, across the hall from his cousin's—Roger Winterslip was away on business—and once the formalities were concluded, the three sat at a small, round conference table.

"Mr. Chan, I want to thank you for making such a long journey to interest yourself in our affairs; really, such kindness on your part. And Mr. Winterslip, your cousin Roger is such a friend to the university . . . " No stranger to extended extemporaneous speaking, Bernardo began to wander from pleasantry to platitude, even firing a short salvo of Latin at his audience of two, before Chan interrupted.

"I am indeed honored to make the acquaintance of one so distinguished in learning, and I hope that my efforts, however slight, may help our friend"—he nodded at Winterslip—"relieve your burden. Perhaps, please, you can explain the trouble that caused you concern?"

The academic pulled pipe and tobacco pouch from a side pocket of his tweed jacket—*These chaps must be required to wear tweed at all times*, Winterslip thought—and paused before preparing to indulge.

"I hope you don't mind, Inspector? Some call it a foul habit, but I find the fumes conducive to thought."

"Please, be at your ease and partake," Chan smiled. "I am not a disciple of so-called goddess Nicotina, but neither am I one to deny others their devotion."

The dean gratefully performed the usual ritual, and Witherspoon lit a cigarette.

"Now, then, Inspector Chan, let me begin again. The money—it's only part of the problem, you see—"

"Please pardon the interruption. Before you describe other parts of the problem, how much money is involved?"

"It's difficult to say exactly. Not my line of country, finance. I have noticed recently, with increasing frequency, an 'unavailability' when I've inquired about sums that I'm certain were allocated to my keeping and disposition, definitely within my purview. Blasted impudence, I call it."

He paused to tend the pipe and launched several streams of fragrant smoke toward the ceiling, adding to an already somewhat cloudy office atmosphere.

"In the beginning it was merely an inconvenience, sometimes a delay in disbursement and nothing more," the dean muttered irritably, his voice faint at first through the growing haze. A furrowed brow drove his distinctive eyebrows lower. (*Reminds one of that old fellow in the talkies,* Winterslip mused.) "But," he said more vigorously, "it's become a pattern, and while I haven't tallied up the numbers it's clear to me that something is awry, and certain sums cannot be found—by me, at any rate. Not just some minor *contretemps*. Possibly even"—he paused for dramatic effect, alternating his words with short, angry draws on his pipe—"dirty work (puff) at the (puff) cross-roads."

"A person who does evil may travel in solitude, but a bad deed never walks alone," Chan said. "Let us conclude that the sum of money lost in mystery is noticeable, but its absence is just one misfortune—as you said, one part of your distress?"

"Eh? Oh, hmm—yes, well," Bernardo paused, in some confusion, his tufted eyebrows returning to their customary resting place. "I'm damned if I know, you'll pardon the inelegant expression. Trouble is," he relit the pipe, which somehow had almost gone out, "there are a hundred different things—most of them quite intangible—that tell me something, someone—maybe more than one someone—is up to something," he concluded weakly.

"I know, believe me." The dean sighed. "It doesn't sound like much, and I'm expressing myself badly—as if it were true what they say about me, some of the younger members of our university community, that I'm an old, hmm,

SOME KIND OF MONEY TROUBLE　　　31

fogey—lost some or all of my wits, time for me to be put out to pasture. Well! I may not be as spry as I once was, but"—he tapped his forehead with the stem of his pipe—"there's nothing wrong upstairs. Of that I can assure you."

"Of course, of course," Winterslip interjected soothingly. "That's why—the uncertainty here—that's why I thought Mr. Chan would be the right person to delve into this situation. I'm sure he can help get to the bottom of it. Why, you're probably familiar with his work over the years—the San Francisco papers have been filled with his doings."

The dean, having read nothing for many years printed later than the sixteenth century, looked puzzled, but recovered gracefully.

"Quite so, quite so. Anything you and Roger recommend, naturally, I endorse. And I want to do what I can to help, but I don't see how I can point Mr. Chan in the right direction without stirring things up on campus. Fact of the matter is, I'm not sure which is the proper direction."

"Sometimes," Chan suggested gently. "The way reveals itself to those who practice 'not doing,' as the ancient philosophers have written. For now, it is enough that we have spoken—to give us some indications—and these we will discuss and pursue as events unfold.

"With utmost discretion," he added quickly, seeing that Dean Bernardo was about to speak.

"You read my mind, Mr. Chan," the old academic said gratefully. "And I will give the matter additional thought. Perhaps I can find a discreet course open to your inquiries.

"In any case," Bernardo added as he made ready to depart, "you can come to campus to call on your daughter without arousing too much suspicion, I dare say."

"Such is my intent, at least for one or two more such visits," said Chan. "Too many appearances by middle-aged Chinese detective might give rise to unwelcome speculation. And if your intuition is correct, better that we do not alarm one who fears discovery—not yet.

"It is not wise to strike a flea that sits on the head of a tiger."

CHAPTER IV

CALLING ON AN OLD FRIEND

"Well? What did you think?"

Winterslip lit another cigarette while Chan looked around at the office and its personal touches: modern artwork adorned two walls, and the young man's desk was populated with a blotter, pen and ink, a small stack of books, and a few framed photos whose subjects he could not identify with a cursory glance.

"Matters are now transparent like virgin soil after arrival of spring rain," Chan replied mischievously.

"Oh—'clear as mud,'" Winterslip laughed. "Yes, I have to agree with you, as to the details. But the old boy clearly has *something* on his mind. And he surely knows that sums of money are evaporating somehow. As for the other concerns—"

"As I told you so many years ago, Chinese people are great believers in psychic ability and earthly intuition," the detective said thoughtfully. "So I am not inclined to dismiss vague feelings of unease that trouble this academic gentleman. Missing money—that is bad, but mistakes can happen even in place populated by extensively educated people with many degrees. What we do not know, and need to explore, is some connection between funds that disappear—and distressed dean. Maybe there is no relationship between these two concerns. But if there is . . ."

"Then you—and I mean we—will really have our work cut out for us," finished Winterslip with a sigh. "Blast Roger for his community mindedness and philanthropic spirit!"

"No need to consign cousin to fiery punishment just yet," Chan replied. "It still may be that the fates will look kindly on us—and the university. But," he added briskly, "fates do not favor the idle, and seeds of investigation must be watered, the soil tilled. We must seek other sources of information and talk to as many university persons as possible to see what can be learned about both money and mood. Maybe others know more about vanishing dollars or have, like the dean, psychic thoughts about campus atmosphere."

"Ok, but how do we do that without swatting that flea you mentioned to the dean—and all the while being discreet? Seems like a tall order."

"You are smart young man, yes? And it is known that your worthy cousin holds a high office in the councils of the university?"

"Well, he's a member of the board—and a big donor," Winterslip smiled. "I guess that's generally known."

"Then you seek meeting with president of university and explain that cousin has tasked you with studying university through conversations on campus with many persons—all for benign purpose. Maybe to determine what university needs most that your cousin can support with future generosity?"

"Say," cried Winterslip, "that's an idea! With a story like that, I should be able to get someone there to talk." He reflected briefly. "But won't they think I'm an awful fool asking questions when, after all, I know practically nothing about the inner workings of a university?"

"One who asks a question may seem to be a fool for five minutes, but if he asks no questions at all he will be a fool forever," Chan replied cheerfully. "And you are no fool."

"Thanks for the compliment," Winterslip laughed. "I'll mention to all that I meet that I am not a fool, perhaps by way of introduction. Anyway, this might not be terribly difficult—getting people to tell me what's wrong if they think that I might be able to help fix it. After all, who wants to stand in the way of progress—and a big donation? But what happens when Roger decides not to make good on this fable of philanthropy?"

"Much may happen before indefinite talk of same is expected to become reality," said Chan. "Meanwhile, you are following cousin Roger's instructions to help university and its dean as originally instructed."

"I suppose you're right," Winterslip admitted, "but what are you going to be doing while I'm stumbling about, asking questions about money and psychic feelings? You are the actual detective, after all, while I," he grinned facetiously, "am merely the beloved amateur of detective fiction. You're the expert!"

Chan smiled. "Like fictional detective, I will not confide in my 'sidekick,' as son Henry refers to junior colleague, just yet. But please be assured that I will not sit still in meditation. I have much to do that may shed some light. Maybe I am not like the modern investigator who bustles about, always probing, questioning—but together, we will need time as well as effort. A river does not freeze in one day."

"Especially not in San Francisco," Winterslip agreed. "I just hope we find some ice soon."

***

Charlie Chan paused in the hallway. The painted lettering on the door's frosted glass confirmed his destination: "J.V. Kirk, Assistant United States Attorney. Please Knock." Before he could do so, the door opened abruptly, revealing a man in a rumpled suit on his way out. Coming face to face with Chan, he mumbled a hasty apology and departed, leaving the door ajar.

Knocking lightly on the open door, the detective stood in the entrance and looked within. A dark-eyed woman at a desk piled high with stacks of documents looked up from a hefty legal volume, peering over the top of reading glasses. "Yes? Oh—surely not! Is it you? Mr. Chan?" As inquiry turned to recognition, June Kirk rose with a laugh, making her way around the desk to clasp both her visitor's hands. "I can't believe it—you, here, in San Francisco?"

"My heart leaps joyously at reunion with friend and colleague from past years," Chan said with a smile, shaking her hands in return. "I hope that I do not intrude on your duties, coming unannounced and unexpected?"

"No, no—not at all," she cried. "This is the highlight of my day—my entire week—but come in, sit down!"

Chan complied. Resuming her seat behind the desk, Kirk peppered him with questions. Why was he here? How long was his stay? Was he free for dinner with her and husband Barry?

"So many questions—is this how you cross-examine unlucky witnesses in court?" Chan smiled. "Allow me to respond without benefit of counsel—I am here for at least several days, to explore confidential matter at the request of old friend while I also enjoy visits with daughter Rose and other persons I recall fondly from previous encounters.

"Foremost of these," he added, "are you and your esteemed spouse—namesake of my youngest son, Barry—

I trust he enjoys continued good health?"

"He does, and he'll be thrilled to see you again," said June Kirk happily. "Both of us have such fond memories of how we met you, and—of course—each other. It seems like just yesterday. How is little Barry? And the rest of the family?"

"Barry Chan serves as constant reminder of your husband, especially each year when the anniversary of his birth recalls to mind the origin of his given name—and my association with you and Mr. Barry Kirk those several years ago."

The attorney smiled. She had been deputy district attorney J.V. Morrow when the case of Sir Frederic Bruce brought her to Chan's attention several years ago, and the former Scotland Yard detective's murder had resulted in both a puzzling case successfully concluded—and a wedding. She had followed up her role in the Bruce homicide investigation by accepting an offer from the U.S. Attorney. The federal role was both an advancement in her career, and a tacit acknowledgement that opportunities for her were limited at the D.A.'s office; she had advanced as far as she cared too in the practice of criminal law. But Chan knew that her professional experience and position in San Francisco society—as the wife of Barry Kirk—boded well in his quest for information.

"Yes, I certainly can say that the Bruce case was my most memorable so far." She laughed. "Not many attorneys find career success *and* matrimony in a single investigation. And you—you haven't changed a bit. But there must be a story behind this sudden visit. You're not investigating the Department of Justice, I hope?"

Chan grinned. "Federal government is safe from my humble efforts, I am happy to report. So glad to renew our acquaintance and friendship, and allow me to congratulate you on the rising prominence of your professional success."

"Thanks, Mr. Chan. But you didn't come here just to celebrate my achievements—how can I help a famous detective?"

Chan acknowledged the compliment with a slight bow. "Kind words warm this moment like sun that burns away city fog, and assistant U.S. attorney is, as son Henry would say, 'Right on the money.' I am here to ask for your unofficial help in confidential investigation."

Briefly, Chan outlined the situation, describing the areas he hoped to explore with her help. Uppermost in his mind, information about the university's financial situation from the outside in, and any potential entrée—a booster, donor, alumnus—that would provide some discreet insight into the subject of his inquiry.

"I am forced to admit that my request to you lacks the specific and concrete nature so important to legal probes, but sometimes casting even an imperfect net widely catches some small fish. And present circumstances demand that I look for even the lowly minnow."

Kirk nodded. "I understand the predicament. You're like a doctor who's been asked to cure a disease without talking to the patient. I think I can help, and of course I'm glad to do what I can. Let me give the matter a little thought and make a few calls. Perhaps Barry and I can take you to dinner—tomorrow night—and we can discuss this, after you and Barry reminisce about old times?"

"I am grateful for your understanding and assistance—and, if events allow, the prospect of a shared meal with your greatly esteemed husband. Truly, this is a fortunate time for visiting detective who arrives unannounced and prevails on previous acquaintance."

CALLING ON AN OLD FRIEND   39

"Mr. Chan, I sometimes think that if you hadn't been with us at the time, Sir Frederic's killer would have escaped. And I," she said with a smile, "might have ended up an old maid! So, please consider yourself a welcome guest in San Francisco and at the Kirk residence always and forever."

The detective bowed his thanks. "I take my leave so that you can attend to more pressing duties. And any message you leave at the Chancellor Hotel, Powell Street, will find me.

"Thank you . . . very much."

Outside of President Emerson's well-appointed office, Castor and Pollux were cleaning and polishing the presidential antechamber's ornate woodwork. The fumes were strong, but Emerson's secretary, a Miss Crandall, ignored the odor and the two workmen, who conversed softly in Welsh.

"You've missed a spot," Castor murmured. "Mind your work."

"I mind that you're a great pot calling a kettle black," Pollux retorted. "See there—you've missed a big patch yourself, long as *Llanfairpwllgwyngyllgogerychwyrndrobwllllantysiliogogogoch*."

The burst of syllables briefly attracted the attention of Miss Crandall, whose scant knowledge of Celtic languages and the geography of Wales left her ill-equipped to interpret this insult. Her glare at the two, however, spoke in the universal language of librarians and schoolmarms— and they took the hint.

"Talk, talk, talk," Castor returned softly, applying an oily rag to the spot in question. "If you were so inclined, perhaps we might talk less and hear more, if you catch my meaning."

"Thanks very much for fitting me into your schedule; really, it's very good of you to see me."

John Quincy Winterslip leaned forward from a leather-back chair to discard cigarette ash nervously into an Argy-Rousseau ashtray. President Emerson faced his visitor from behind an imposing desk and attempted to put him at ease.

"Not at all, Mr. Winterslip. Only too glad to assist in a matter like this, especially to extend every courtesy to your cousin. Not only is he a trustee, he's a loyal friend of the university. Such inquiries," he affected the self-assured mien of a head of state, "do arise from time to time, but this degree of interest—I should say, this particular method of personal inquiry, is unusual. What is it, exactly, that you propose to do on our campus to advance Roger's interests?"

Winterslip paused to recall exactly how Chan had phrased it, how to make it sound plausible.

"Well, you see, Roger has so many business duties which demand his attention that he can't attend to the matter himself—in fact, he's out of town at present—and he thought that I might do what he would like to do himself, if he had the time." Seeing Emerson's puzzled expression, he rattled on quickly: "That is, to just talk to as many faculty and staff—perhaps even a few students—as possible. The idea being to hear what the university needs most and then, perhaps, to act on those needs. In a generous way. No guarantee of course, but this first step is necessary for Roger to . . . inquire into the possibilities."

The president inhaled deeply and expelled the breath slowly, tapping a pencil on the arm of his chair. His thoughts raced, but his face was a mask of avuncular concern for the younger man wasting presidential time with this

CALLING ON AN OLD FRIEND 41

proposed . . . fishing expedition. Hours of faculty meetings had made him something of an expert in dissimulation. He had often thoughtthat he might make an excellent poker player, but his lofty position precluded socializing with those who would consider cards a suitable pastime.

"But why not simply consult me? I could certainly share all manner of urgent and future needs here that could be addressed by a philanthropic individual such as Roger Winterslip. In fact, I've already discussed some of these priorities with him and the other members of the board."

John Quincy rose to the challenge.

"Ah, yes—of course! Roger did brief me on the view from the top, so to speak. But he wants to add to that—no disrespect to you, of course!—he wants to combine your priorities with the views of, you'll pardon the expression, lesser mortals. Not that they would disagree with their president," he added hastily, fearing he had offended the academic potentate. "No doubt I would find a great deal of support for your way of thinking. My sense is—Roger's sense is—that this exercise, these conversations with the rank-and-file, would not only add fuel to your fire, but maybe, just maybe, mind you, I might be able to discover some lesser needs that haven't come to your attention. Things that people feel keenly, not huge institutional matters, but important to them in their daily duties, so to speak, that could be addressed with the application of," he paused for breath, "generous donor support."

Emerson smiled and glanced at a wall clock, signaling that a president's time—even when discussing possible donor support—was not limitless.

"I think I have a better understanding of what you have in mind, and I have no objection at all. Naturally, you must expect a certain amount of reticence from individuals at an academic institution. Please indicate that you have my support in your . . . research. But be prepared for varying degrees of cooperation. Even some reluctance, possibly."

He rose to indicate that the interview was over, and Winterslip followed suit, extinguishing what remained of his cigarette and shaking the proffered presidential hand.

"Do keep me apprised of your progress, and please give my best to your cousin."

A presidential secretary opened the door and reminded Emerson of an appointment in Sacramento as Winterslip exited the office. The amateur detective walked quickly to his nearby roadster and sped away to his office.

Gad, he thought, driving from the campus back to the real world. *What drivel I spouted—and what a pompous ass of a president! I wonder if he's somehow in the middle of this muddle?*

It was a question that John Quincy would recall again. And again.

CHAPTER V

TEA AND REMINISCENCE

The Locus Bonum café, not far from the university, was both a coffee house and a tavern. Mornings were generally given over to hot drinks designed to fortify patrons against the rigors of the coming day, and the atmosphere was one of quiet, studious solitude—mostly solo customers absorbing the latest newspapers along with their cups of coffee (and tea, and even chocolate). Daily papers, weeklies—and a few recent magazines—were racked on a wall near the bar.

But it was now late afternoon, and the venue was transforming into the louder, more boisterous gathering place that attracted both students and faculty well into the evenings, some for spirited intellectual debate; others, to celebrate (or commiserate) while downing beer and strong drink. Tobacco smoke from cigarettes, pipes and a few cigars further darkened the dimly lit interior.

In a corner of the room, three men were arguing at a small table littered with more than one empty bottle and an overflowing ashtray. From time to time, one or more of the trio looked around to see if anyone was paying attention to them. Other patrons appeared to be tending to their own affairs, but it was best to be certain.

"I am fed up with the arrogance of my so-called 'colleagues,'" Gilvie Silva hissed, crushing the last of one cigarette and lighting another. "Their ignorance of the international situation—of *our* situation—competes with their arrogance. Either they know little or nothing of what happens abroad, or they dismiss events brought to their attention. They say America has no business interfering—a coward's argument!"

His colleague, a slight Filipino sporting a most unacademic MacIntosh suit, was not impressed. "Talk, talk, talk—and always about places far away. What do you say, and what can we do, about here? Injustice, greed, folly—they happen not only in Europe, where things are very bad now—these things are here, in this city, this place." Eduardo Dimayuga, professor of chemistry, whose third glass of beer had loosened his tongue and sharpened his oratory, preferred immodestly to be called *Bayani*, "hero," because his given name reminded him of Spain's heel on the neck of his forebearers.

Jacques Marc, a professor of French, poured the last of a carafe of cabernet into his glass. "No doubt it is as you both say—but what can men do if they cannot go and fight?"

Silva smiled grimly.

"People die now far from here, and America thinks it cannot happen in this country—it is not their affair. What if," he produced two nearly perfect smoke rings over the heads of his companions, "violence, even death, came here, in some fashion—to shake these damned *gilipollas*? Wake them up!"

Dimayuga frowned. "What you say there, I cannot agree. To shock the Americans into action, that is one thing. But to kill—" He shook his head.

"Let us not quarrel," Silva retorted dismissively.

TEA AND REMINISCENCE 45

"We all have our work to do. And it may be that events will overtake us all."

Deep into the night, Provost Merriweather lay awake, revisiting his plan. For quite a long time, he had been channeling anger into a definite strategy. A disinterested observer would have called his attitude obsessive, but he did not concern himself with the opinions of others. In fact, he suspected that he was generally held in contempt by the university community; rejection of his presidential bid was, he felt, evidence of that. And he returned their lack of regard. Many—no, most of the faculty were contemptible, their weak scholarship proof of intellectual poverty.

He did not consider himself an aggressive man, but he was now convinced that the success of his strategy depended on a departure from norms. A career academic, he considered himself a rational thinker. But dwelling on perceived injustice had overcome mental resistance to increasing thoughts of direct action. He had planned long enough—the time had come.

Tomorrow would be here soon, a few hours' sleep would do him no harm—if he could only still the raging torrent of angry thoughts. His sleep, when it came, was fitful.

Dawn arrived, and he looked forward to what the day might bring.

Arising at his accustomed time, Charlie Chan breakfasted again in the hotel dining room. With Winterslip assigned the difficult task of probing the academic community, the detective had decided on his morning's itinerary. First, a call on his cousin in Chinatown; second, a stop at the venerable San Francisco Public Library for some research; and then, a visit to Rose at the provost's office. Although he wanted to limit his presence on campus, a brief stop by a visiting father taking his daughter to lunch should, he thought, not attract attention from any suspicious persons. By afternoon, he hoped, a second conversation with June Kirk might provide additional threads to weave into a slowly developing tapestry; with what result, he could not say. But it was still early, and there was—potentially—much to discover.

For the detective, who had felt the pull of two ways of life for many years, a visit to Chinatown was always a strange experience, a contrast between rooted ancient culture and the creep of modern influences. Chan typically began with a walk along Grant Avenue, which he found to be an amusing barometer of change—one could see, over time, the extent to which Chinatown's forward-facing main street was becoming less and less authentic.

In fact, as Chan observed, this avenue of entry to Chinatown was somewhat less Chinese. In addition to the steadily increasing intrusion of American-style commercial offerings—neon signs, restaurants serving both American and Chinese dishes—the Japanese had found several footholds along the avenue. Chan noted with some distaste the presence of these pretenders, with goods "Made in Japan" in shops tended by Japanese. Apparently, he thought sadly, the Emperor and generals are eager for conquest even in this San Francisco district.

Thankfully, true to his previous visits, the farther north he walked the more familiar and genuine Chinatown became. Authentic culture, seemingly transplanted from his native Canton, still held its own in this urban enclave surrounded by American influences Not far off Grant, the lesser streets were more to his liking, including his destination, Waverly Place.

Recalling his cousin's sharp comment from a previous visit about loud knocking, Charlie Chan tapped gently on the door, and in a moment Chan Kee Lim opened it slowly.

"Greetings, my cousin, and my apologies for this intrusion," Chan said in somewhat rusty Cantonese. "As you see, the way that I walk has brought me again to your city."

"Cousin, you are always welcome," Kee Lim answered in their native tongue. "Deign to enter my modest abode." He gestured to his visitor, opening the door wide. "Sit and be at home, as though we were again in the country of our ancestors." Chan So, Kee Lim's wife, made an appearance, bowing in welcome, and departed the room to prepare tea.

Preliminaries dispensed with, the two exchanged inquiries as to the health of absent family members and observed other ritual niceties suitable to the occasion. Chan noticed that his cousin had grayed considerably since their last meeting. Chan So returned with an elegant Chinese tea service, and the two men partook.

"Your hospitality shines with the light of many suns, and I am honored to be so received," Chan remarked.

"Your visits are welcome but too infrequent," Kee Lim returned. "Yet your daughter's presence reminds my household of the familial bonds. It pleases me to share with you that she is a credit to the family of Chan and our ancestors. Also," he added, "she and her cousin of the same name bring joy to Chan So, as women do with their female kin."

The outer door to the apartment opened, and the two Roses entered, chatting happily in English.

"Ah, Li Mei—please pay your respects to our famous cousin from the islands," Kee Lim told his daughter sharply. Ignoring the girls' burst of English, he continued to speak in Cantonese. "Let us observe courtesy in my household, and perhaps even speak as my fathers spoke."

Kee Lim's daughter bowed to the detective, and they exchanged traditional greetings, but she quickly switched back to English. "Rose and I just stopped for a moment to say hello. We're off to the library to study, and I don't have to work till this afternoon."

"Filial duty and family greeting—your attention to these is noteworthy," Chan remarked, nodding at his daughter. "And such dedication to your educational pursuits—are these two younger ones not good examples of virtuous thinking and right acting, cousin?"

A short burst of Cantonese from Kee Lim made it plain that he did not approve: of the younger generation's behavior, generally; of too much English contaminating his household; and of education aimed at modern goals. "Better that they should devote more time to the classics, the rites—the teachings of the old masters," he grumbled. "And they speak inelegantly, in the words of the common American people."

"Don't let Dad fool you, honored cousin." Kee Lim's daughter grinned. "He actually speaks English pretty good—and understands even more than he speaks. He just likes to play the part of the ancient sage." Both Roses giggled, and Kee Lim frowned.

"Remember—remember these words from long ago," Chan interjected, hoping to soothe Kee Lim's irritation. "Always be aware of the age of your parents, because it is cause for both joy *and* sorrow."

"You speak true words, cousin." Kee Lim was some-what mollified. Reference to the classics—especially from someone as contaminated by the West as the famous detective—proved that he had won this skirmish, at least.

The two students departed, and the men returned to tea and reminiscence. It had been many years since they had come to the West, but the bonds of childhood and family from a far-off time were fresh in their shared memories. And despite Kee Lim's prickly exterior, Chan found him sincere, honest, upright—and not without humor, although he rarely laughed.

An hour passed. Glancing at his watch, Chan made ready to leave.

"With regret, I must take my leave from your gracious household," he told his host, bowing. "Mere words seem insufficient to thank you for extending hospitality—not just to me, but to my Rose as well."

Kee Lim bowed low in return, and answered in a mix of Cantonese and English. "It is well, cousin. I am older than you, and joy fills me to see the two younger branches of our tree grow close. Good for them. Good for Chan family. For future."

Chan bowed a second time, and departed.

Even as Chan pursued his line of investigation at the public library, Rose and Li Mei immersed themselves in the university library stacks for the better part of an hour. They had settled at opposite ends of a long oaken study table, books scattered between and around them. A few other students came and went, but it was still early— for most undergraduates—and the quiet atmosphere was conducive to intellectual pursuits.

Until the explosion.

Rose would later describe the sound as "louder than a door slamming, not as loud as a clap of thunder," but at the moment it occurred, she and Li Mei were jolted as though a giant hand had nudged the building. Shouts and cries of "Fire!" followed in short order, and the two Chans ran toward the building entrance, joined by a dozen or more students and others—staff, and maybe faculty, Rose thought—all of them spilling out of the doorway and onto the lawn. The smell of smoke preceded wisps that emerged from the rear of the building, but no fire could be seen, at least not right away.

The stunned evacuees talked excitedly in small groups, the crowd quickly growing with other students and faculty from neighboring buildings responding to the noise. In a few minutes sirens announced the arrival of both fire and police departments.

Chan's time at the public library was less eventful and more productive. He left, with more than one train of thought set in motion by the last hour's research, and made his way to the university campus to call on Rose at the provost's office. But the commotion outside the library, and the presence of the authorities, prompted a change in course.

"Over here, Dad!" Rose had spotted her approaching parent, distinctive in appearance from the rest of the gathering crowd, and he hurried to her side. In a few words, the two students explained the noise, "an explosion—like a bomb," and assured him that they were unhurt. The three watched as fire crews uncoiled a hose and ran it along the side of the building toward the smoke. Police had moved the onlookers further away from the building, and the curious continued to arrive—a dozen students and faculty including Professor Silva and Provost Merriweather, both somewhat out of breath.

"What's happened? Is everyone all right? I heard something in my office—sounded like a chap of thunder—

ran all the way—"

"Too soon to know, surely," Gertrude Winget interrupted from behind Merriweather. She must have followed in his wake, thought Chan, but she appeared more composed, less disheveled than the provost. Silva, he noticed, seemed agitated, hands clasping and unclasping, his dark eyes shifting their gaze from colleagues, to firefighters, to the building and back again. Even though the cause of the blast and smoke was unknown, the detective's observations and instincts were already inclined to categorize everyone at the scene as likely or unlikely suspects. His belief that "Chinese people are psychic," which Rose had heard many times over the years, was asserting itself.

Charlie Chan had no crystal ball, but instinct and experience told him this was no accident. Was it somehow a response to his presence on campus, to his "confidential" investigation?

He wondered.

CHAPTER VI
A SHARP CRY

Eventually the smoke cleared, and police and fire personnel sounded the all clear. Students and other onlookers still milled about, eager to be part of a most un-collegiate event. For undergraduates, it was the most exciting thing to have happened on the campus, definitely more interesting than hitting the books. Some of the adults on the scene were not as enthusiastic.

"Aye, who do you suppose will be cleanin' up this mess all the summer long?" Castor posed the rhetorical question to Pollux; the two had been otherwise—and separately—occupied halfway across campus when they heard the booming noise. Now, they stood apart from the gaggle of onlookers and evaluated the unseen damage behind the smoke, adding to it with a shared cigarette.

"Mun, hold your complainin' till this thing is sorted," his fellow Poovey said sharply. "A bad business, this is. I'm hopin' there's no one hurt."

"Truth be told, I think there's more smoke here than fire, and more noise than blast, if you take my meanin'," Castor replied matter-of-factly.

"Now, then, have you all of a sudden become an expert on such things?" Pollux needled. "I'll make a note of it—your knowledge grows day to day, I'll be bound. It must be that you're soaking it up from all these highly eddicated folk."

"Have your bit of fun, then. We'll soon see who knows what when the time comes." Castor crushed the last bit of their cigarette with his heel for emphasis.

"No holdin' back information obtained," Pollux reminded him sharply. "Have you perhaps heard somethin' of interest—somethin' you'd care to pass along to your comrade here?"

"Not a bit of it," the other returned. "It's just that I have a certain intuition, just like Grandda' used to say—"

Pollux scoffed. "Don't be a-draggin' the honored dead into your pipe dream. And while we're waitin' for the smoke to clear, have you the makings?"

Like a conjurer's trick, tobacco and paper appeared in Castor's rough hands and were transformed into a cigarette sufficient for two.

Nearby, Charlie Chan huddled with Rose and their cousin, both young women still shaken by their experience. The provost, having consulted with the police officer in charge, was eager to act. He approached the detective.

"Mr. Chan, I realize that you are here as a visiting parent, but would you please indulge me? I've asked Miss Winget to find the library director and bring him to my office to discuss what comes next, and having someone of your investigative talents present will be most helpful, I'm sure. This is hardly the place for a private conversation."

Chan nodded, and suggested to the two Roses that they meet later at Locus Bonum, the nearby café-tavern. "Make sure you solve this mystery fast," his daughter warned. "We were in the thick of it, and we want to know what happened."

Chan grimaced. "Eager offspring has apparently

inherited parental curiosity, but please remember that moving a mountain begins with the small stones—and we do not yet know how big is this mountain."

A short walk across campus brought the detective to the provost's office, where a half-dozen university administrators were gathered around a long table with the provost at the head. Chan removed his hat, bowed slightly to the gathering, and took a seat.

Gordon Merriweather cleared his throat and began. "Thank you for gathering on such short notice—" he glanced at his watch. "I had asked Gertrude to join us to take notes of our discussion so that we might have a record of this meeting, but she must be otherwise occupied, so I will perform that office. Some of you may be familiar with the reputation of Inspector Charlie Chan, who's here visiting his daughter, a student who works in my office. I asked Mr. Chan to join us for this meeting, informally. Of course the police will be looking into the matter officially."

Chan nodded in acknowledgement of the introduction. The provost looked quickly around the table before proceeding.

"Dean Bernardo must have been delayed, but we can brief him when he arrives," he noted. "I've spoken to President Emerson by telephone; he's in Sacramento on university business, and he has asked me to take charge of the situation. Fortunately, the police assure me that no one has been seriously hurt. A few persons were troubled by the smoke, and they were evaluated by medical personnel—nothing worse than that."

Chan interjected. "Pardon the interruption, please. Officials have had first look at inside of library—have they said anything to you about the cause of loud noise and smoke that followed?"

The provost frowned. "The officer I spoke to was unclear on that point, Mr. Chan. It seems that the, hmm, point of origin was at or near a boiler on the ground floor of the library. But they have not determined whether there was a device, a—"

"Bomb?" Chan suggested.

"The police have not used that word, and they appeared to me to be truly uncertain." He turned to the head librarian. "Mr. Ellison, they asked me about the condition of the boiler, its age and so on."

Ellison was a slight, owlish man whose crumpled attire and uncombed hair had not been caused by the disturbance at the library. Colleagues and students could attest that he always appeared to have been dragged through a hedge backwards.

"Quite old, as old as the library itself," he said mournfully. "Definitely due for replacement. I was able to have a look at the damage, which was confined to the rear of the building. It's an area not frequented by staff or patrons, really a service and maintenance room, and there was very little fire, mostly smoke and some water damage from both the contents of the boiler, and an abundance of caution on the part of the fire brigade, which assumed that there was more fire than was the case."

Merriweather nodded. "I'm sure that the police will know more soon, and—unfortunately—the library will remain closed until their investigation has concluded. And then, of course, there will be the matter of airing the smoke-infested portions of the building, restoring heat and hot water—I presume the boiler is damaged beyond repair, but I leave that to you to determine—"

The door opened abruptly to admit Dean Bernardo, flustered as usual—perhaps more so as a result of this unseemly disruption to the life of the institution. He stood and stared at the three men.

"Beg pardon, I'm sure, Dr. Merriweather, please excuse my tardy arrival—'pon my word, this is beyond the pale, one distressing event after another, and—"

"Quite so, and we are all very much disturbed, Dean Bernardo," the provost agreed smoothly. I was just sharing what we know so far: no one badly hurt, minimal damage, the cause of the, hmm, explosion not yet known. And the library, as you would expect, is going to be closed for the time being. Won't you have a seat?"

Chan observed their exchange with some curiosity. Bernardo blinked, uncertainty flitting across his face. "The library? But surely—" He sank heavily into a chair, grasping its arms with hands just visible at the ends of his customary robe's sleeves. "That is, I was about to say—of course." He paused and looked down for a moment. "Please, continue with your discussion. I apologize again for arriving late."

"Not at all," Merriweather replied. *Really*, he thought, *the old boy seems dottier than ever. If I were president, the academic administration here would soon see some new blood. And fancy Emerson being out of town when the university needs leadership! That won't look well to the board, or the faculty.* His reverie lasted no more than a few seconds, and ended when Chan respectfully raised a hand.

"Again, I ask pardon for interrupting, but as concerned parent I now beg leave to depart—would like to see daughter and cousin who were in the library when unfortunate event occurred."

Merriweather nodded.

"Thank you, Mr. Chan, for joining our colloquy. The university is fortunate to have such a distinguished visitor, albeit in an unofficial capacity." Chan rose and bowed to the group. The others made ready to follow him.

The detective's hand was on the doorknob when a sharp cry penetrated the office walls. Chan and the others rushed from the room in the direction of a second inarticulate sound, a muffled scream followed by silence. It was clear that the noises had come from a room just down the hall from the provost's office, its door ajar. Chan arrived first, with the others close behind. Pushing the door open, he could see enough to caution the rest to come no further. He entered the room and closed the door behind him.

Gertrude Winget stood in the center of the room, staring fixedly at its only other occupant. A woman lay on her side, facing the wall, on a long runner rug with a red floral pattern that camouflaged some, if not all, of the blood from a head wound—the cause of which was all too apparent. An ornate academic mace, its decorative metal head dented and marred by a small, dull-red stain, rested nearby. Treading lightly around a tableau of rug, body, desk and chair, Chan felt for a pulse and found none. He rose and turned to Winget.

"This woman is dead—you entered the room just now?" The provost's secretary was without her usual composure and its constant companion, efficiency. She struggled to find words.

"Oh no—this is dreadful. It's—she—"

"Dead woman is known to you?"

"I can't see her face, but I think it's a member of the faculty . . . Stark, Mildred Stark. If I could just see her face, to be sure—" she moved toward the body, but Chan spoke sharply.

"Touch nothing, please! Confirmation of identity can wait, but now we must notify police. I request, please, that you do so, and ask others outside this door to remain in hallway."

Winget stared blankly at Chan for a moment, then turned and left the room to carry out his instructions.

Knowing that time was precious, the detective knelt carefully by the corpse clad in an academic robe, looking closely at the main visible injury, to the right eye and the front of the scalp, its gray hair matted, and the left check smeared with dried blood. The victim had been, he thought, about five-and-a-half feet tall. Without touching the body, he scanned it and its surroundings thoroughly; the smeared blood on the face and some scuff marks on the long rug drew his attention.

The room was a large, windowless former classroom. More recently, it had served as an office and storage area. Some previous occupant's desk and chair remained, along with a floor lamp that was the only source of light. Along one wall, dozens of black academic robes hung limply on a long rack, and the opposite wall showcased university paraphernalia on floor-to-ceiling wooden bookshelves. Behind the desk hung three oil paintings, portraits of past university presidents. On the desk several books lay scattered, and Chan noted works of fiction—older English literature, mostly—some he knew, others were unfamiliar. He pulled out notebook and pencil, and jotted down the titles.

"Hey—you there!"

A uniformed officer stood in the doorway, the provost, dean and Gertrude Winget peering over his shoulder.

"I'm Mallory, from headquarters," the burly officer announced. "Homicide is on its way, and until then nobody touches nothin'—clear?"

Chan stood to one side as Officer Mallory approached the body, and delivered a sweeping glance that ended on the detective.

"Now, just for the record, who are you and how long have you been here?" Mallory's pad and pencil stub had emerged from a uniform breast pocket.

"My name is Charlie Chan, and I came to this room from down the hall when this lady"—he gestured toward Winget—"cried for help, perhaps 15 minutes ago."

"Yeah? And what were you doin' down the hall—a bit old to be a student, ain'tcha?"

Chan grinned. "Officer's observation correct like arrow that finds bullseye. This middle-aged Chinese is present in the guise of parent who visits member of university staff, my daughter Rose."

"Is that so?" Mallory's pencil paused, his skepticism clear. "And where's this daughter of yours? I've already seen this lady, and her boss—where's this daughter you were visiting?"

"Here!" Rose Chan arrived, somewhat out of breath—she had run down the hall after hearing the news—"I'm Rose Chan, and I work in the provost's office. And he's my father."

"Ok, ok, just getting everything straight." Mallory shooed the group away from the doorway and closed the door. "Somebody got a key to this door?"

"I have, officer." Winget produced a brass key, and Mallory secured the crime scene. "Now, then, I'll need a room, somewhere close, big enough for all of us to wait till help shows up."

Led by Winget, the dean and provost, Chan, Rose and Mallory made their way into a nearby classroom; the provost was not happy at being herded with the hoi polloi.

"You, Officer—"

"Mallory,"

"—Officer Mallory, I must protest. I am acting on

behalf of the president of the university, and I demand to see the officer in charge. Your superior. Now."

Out came the official notepad. "Your name?"

The provost glared as though any mere mortal, on or off campus, should know his identity without inquiring. "Gordon . . Merriweather," he began slowly, to accommodate the struggles of Mallory's stubby penmanship. "Provost—" the pencil wavered uncertainly; Merriweather sniffed and added icily: "Chief. Academic. Officer. And president *pro tempore*."

The Latin proved too much for Mallory—it was not a phrase he had heard in church—and the notetaking stopped. "Ok, duly noted. I'm just the beat cop securing the scene for now. This lady"—he gestured toward Winget—"she called headquarters, so as for seeing somebody higher up, you will, bub, you will. Just as soon as he gets here. Meanwhile, pipe down and wait your turn.

"Now, everybody, please. I'm going down the hall, but I'll be right back—and no talkin' amongst yourselves." He exited, closing the door with a bang. Some of the internees began to speak, prompting Chan to raise his voice.

"Please! Observe command of official authority and remain silent. Officer wishes to avoid possible witnesses sharing versions of events before initial questioning takes place."

Silence reigned for at least 30 seconds. Then, footsteps approached and the door opened to admit a youngish man with dark, close-cropped hair and a confident bearing, followed by Officer Mallory.

"Ok, like I said, I'm back—and this is Detective Buckley from homicide. He's going to take you one at a time to the room where the body is and ask you some questions. Everybody else will stay here with me till it's their turn."

Buckley stepped forward, assumed a commanding stance, then looked at each member of the group in turn as he spoke, slowly and clearly.

"I know that you're all upset, and I appreciate your cooperation. You probably all know that there's a body in the room down the hall, and anytime there's an unattended death we have to rule out homicide. Or rule it in," he paused for effect, casting his eyes back and forth. "I'm going to ask you"—he pointed to Chan—"to come with me, and the rest of you stay here with Officer Mallory until called for. Any questions?"

"Detective, I am Provost Merriweather, and I am acting on behalf of the president in his absence, and I would like a few words with you—"

Buckley glanced at Mallory, who nodded as if to say, "He's the one I was telling you about."

"Well, Mr. Merriweather—"

"*Provost* Merriweather, please."

"Well, then, *Provost* Merriweather, I appreciate your position here, but for now this is a police matter, *I'm* in charge, and I'll let you know when we can have a little chat. Is that clear?"

The academic fumed inwardly, but knew it was no use to remonstrate further. "Very well," he muttered, and took a seat in the nearest chair.

"I would like—that is, I wonder if it would be possible," began Dean Bernardo, with a pained expression on his face.

"Yes?"

"I should like to visit the gentlemen's wash room— a medical necessity, I assure you, just down the hall—"

"Fine. You do that, and come right back here. Officer Mallory will be stationed outside this room, and he'll be expecting you, so don't go wandering off."

Buckley nodded to the others, and the parade of Mallory, Bernardo and the two detectives departed. While the officer remained outside the door, and the dean performed his errand, Chan followed Buckley to the room with the body.

Buckley closed the door behind them.

"So, Inspector—it is Inspector, right?—Inspector Chan, under other circumstances, I'd be happy to meet you," Buckley began without preamble. "And, yes, I know who you are—saw your picture in the papers the last time you were in town—but the idea of you and a body showing up together seems, well, I don't know how to say it. Not a coincidence? Cause and effect? You tell me."

Chan nodded. "Detective Buckley, I agree that I am like the uninvited guest who appears at a wedding, but my presence here owes much to my daughter's employment at the university. Unlike you, I have no official status and am just one among many you must question to determine what this deceased person represents."

Buckley's tone conveyed his skepticism. "Uh-huh. A good father traveling hundreds of miles just to see his daughter. Sure."

Chan interrupted. "Please excuse my unclear words. Daughter is one reason I am here, but not the only reason." He explained how he had come to combine a family visit with a favor for an old friend, the unofficial financial probe, and Buckley nodded.

"That's more like it. I appreciate you leveling with me. Look, it's not like help from a famous detective would be a bad thing—if you're offering, that is—so maybe you could help me see what we're dealing with here? These college types are a pain, in my experience. And the president of this outfit is friends with the chief, so a little help from you could smooth things over in some quarters. Unofficially, of course."

Chan smiled. "Happy to be of unofficial assistance. May I ask if you have made full examination of room, since I assume coroner has not yet arrived?"

"No, but the coroner happened to be at the station house wrapping up another case, and he should be here soon."

"Then I suggest my first unofficial act will be to assist you in beginning that task—but first, perhaps you wish to see others react to this scene?"

"You're damn right I do," Buckley said grimly. "I like to keep an open mind, but this looks to me like anything but an accident, and I'll bet one of those people knows something that could give us a pointer."

Chan nodded agreement. "The one who points the way sometimes already knows what lies at journey's end."

CHAPTER VII

THE CORONER'S REPORT

"Buckley—I hear you have something of interest for me?"

The two detectives turned to see the coroner, medical bag in hand, in the doorway.

"Doc, nice to see you. Inspector Chan, meet our coroner, Dr. David Chalmers. Dave, this is *the* Charlie Chan." The two men exchanged nods. "And here's your subject." Buckley gestured toward the body. "Tell me it was some kind of accident, and we can all go home."

The coroner smiled, unpacking the tools of his grim trade, and leaned over the corpse. "I'm sure that would make your life easier, but let's see, shall we?" Glancing at the bloody mace and the head wound, he scribbled in a well-worn notebook. "My vast experience tells me that suicide can be ruled out—unless you have a theory of self-inflicted bludgeoning?"

Used to the coroner's morbid wit, Buckley smiled, and yielded the field. The coroner went about his business for a few minutes, then turned to the two detectives.

"Say, give me a hand here. I need to turn her over."

Buckley and Chan grasped arms and legs and gently shifted the body so that it lay face up, and the repositioning revealed a small book, which Chan gingerly retrieved, holding its edges.

"*Sonnets from the Portuguese*," Buckley noted, looking over his shoulder. "Must've been on the desk with the other books—probably fell when she did."

Chan returned the book to the floor. "My desire to look inside this little book is great. Your fingerprint man will be here soon? Please have him examine this book carefully. Leather cover may yield prints, but I do not hold out much hope for such a rough surface."

Buckley nodded. "The lab boys are on their way, and once Doc is done we'll know just how much we want them to do here. But I'm more interested in that fancy club—if anybody was swinging that around, there should be prints on the handle."

Chan glanced at the mace. "True words are not always beautiful, but this 'fancy club' may have much to tell us." The coroner rose from the body, having measured, probed and otherwise performed the duties of his office, and jotted down the results.

"No surprise here. 'Person or persons unknown' is where we're headed. Death appears to have been caused by both blunt force trauma and the wound inflicted by the introduction of at least one of the sharp points on the—top? crown?—of this ceremonial doo-dad into the oculus, resulting in vitreous hemorrhage."

"Doc, Doc—English?"

"Ah—ok, so here's the deal. That, hmm, mace? It makes a good weapon for two reasons: Number one, it's heavy enough to be a club—so she got at least one, probably only one, whack on the forehead. That's the blunt force trauma." Pointing at the top of the mace with his pencil, he continued. "And, number two, the top. It's crenellated," —he held up his hand as Buckley opened his mouth—"a fancy word that means it's like the top of an old castle, jagged edges.

One of those points pierced the left eye and maybe—an autopsy will tell us for sure—entered the brain. Either the whack or the poke in the eye could've killed her, take your pick."

"Thanks for the translation. How about when?"

"Well, less than 12 hours—but you know that's just an educated guess. Tell me how active she was before death, how warm this room was over the last day, and a few other criteria, and I'll be more precise." He flipped his notebook shut. "The rest depends on autopsy, and you'll have my report as soon as—"

"Yeah, yeah. 'As soon as humanly possible.' I've heard that one before. And you've got other stiffs to carve up, no doubt. Thanks, Doc. Always a pleasure. Give my regards to Alice."

On his way out, the coroner exchanged greetings with the fingerprint expert, who entered, unpacked his kit, and went to work. Buckley pointed out the mace and book on the floor as items of special interest. "We'll leave you to it," he said. "Got people down the hall we can't keep waiting any longer." Exiting the room, the two heard angry cries and raised voices, including Officer Mallory's. The door was open, and Mallory stood half in, half out of the room, both hands raised in frustration.

"What's all the squawking about?" Buckley demanded, tapping the officer on the shoulder. The room fell silent for a moment, then a newcomer—it was Professor Silva—repeated his recent objections.

"This officer, he tells me I must wait with these other people—I only stopped to ask what happens here, and he pushes me into the room, like, like—"

"Nobody pushed you, fella," Mallory snapped. "You just needed some encouragement to stay a while." He turned to

Buckley. "This guy shows up and seems a little too curious, and I think maybe he should just wait till you got back, and—"

"Ok, ok, that's fine. And who might you be?"

Buckley's query threatened to unleash another burst of indignation, but Silva swallowed most of his anger and replied briskly. "I am Gilberto Silva, professor at this university, and a free man who objects to this detention. You represent the police?"

"Mallory and I *are* the police," Buckley returned. "So just pipe down till we sort this out. Mr. Chan here has agreed to help me, unofficially, till we see what's what. First thing we need to do is take you, one at a time, down the hall for a little chat. And the rest of you will kindly wait here with the officer." He turned to Silva. "Since you've been treated so badly, professor, how about you go first, and then, hopefully, we can get you out of this?"

Recovering something of his dignity, Silva nodded and straightened his necktie. "I follow you, and these others are my witnesses. Stories of police abusing the people—who has not heard them?" He looked around the room, nodded vigorously, and followed Chan and Buckley.

Mallory closed the door after them. The provost paced, visibly annoyed, and the dean appeared lost in thought. Winget was used to hiding her feelings behind a supportive secretarial mask. Rose Chan recalled how as a girl she had begged her father to take her on an important case so many times, it had become a family joke. Now, her childhood wish had been granted. *At least this has nothing to do with the real reason for Dad's trip*, she said to herself. But just as that reassuring thought arose, doubt followed close behind.

As the daughter of a detective, she knew that the unexpected happened all too often.

Just down the hall, Charlie Chan and Detective Buckley were seated opposite Professor Silva. Buckley flipped open his notebook and began.

"Name, please."

Silva paused, staring defiantly at the two detectives before replying with more than a trace of contempt.

"Gilberto Portillo y Silva. You may address me as 'Professor Silva.'"

"That's fine, fine." Buckley cast a glance at Chan before indicating the silent occupant of the room. "You knew the deceased?"

Silva looked at the uncovered body, swallowed, and returned the detective's steady gaze.

"Professor Stark."

"Describe your relationship with her."

Whatever its intent, the query did not sit well with Silva.

"I find your question, and the tone, and this whole— proceeding, if that is the correct word—beyond insulting. I will not dignify it with an answer."

"Refused to answer," Buckley noted under his breath, jotting the comment into the notebook of record. "So you have nothing to tell us that might shed light on this situation?"

"How can I tell? Certainly I know many things as a professor at this university, but I have no way of knowing which of these might or might not aid you in your investigation." Silva paused, then continued. "As I said, I was in the hall when your officer so rudely thrust me into the room with the others. About this woman and her death, I have no knowledge."

The notebook closed abruptly; Buckley was regretting his decision to begin the questioning with, quite possibly, the least cooperative subject. "Very well, you can go—but we may ask you to expand on your . . . answers."

As Silva got to his feet, Chan raised a hand.

"One moment, please. You are aware of disturbance at library today?"

Silva paused and turned to face his questioner.

"What does that matter have to do with this poor woman? Everyone surely knows of the library incident—it announced itself with something like thunder, did it not? And why," he pointed a finger at Chan, "do you two gentlemen pretend to question me about a body here, then bother me about something that had nothing to do with this? From you," he turned to Buckley, "I would expect such treatment since I am a foreigner. But you," back to Chan, "from one like you, also a stranger in this country, I would expect greater sympathy, if not courtesy."

Chan returned the volley with a bland expression. "My sympathy is for unfortunate woman whose untimely death we investigate. As for courtesy, I forgive somewhat hasty conclusion of yours. Wheel of appearance revolves quickly, and how would you know that I am American citizen, proud to say."

His outraged dignity in tatters, Silva made no reply as he exited the room.

Detective Buckley walked briskly to the door and shouted instructions to Mallory, and the sound of businesslike footsteps in the hall were quickly followed by the arrival of the dean. As might be expected, the aged academic appeared more flustered, blustery and C.-Aubrey-Smith-like than usual. But, for once in his life, he was speechless.

"Now, sir," Buckley addressed the silent dean. "For the record, tell me your name and what you do here."

"B-Bernardo. Aloysius Bernardo. I'm the college dean."

"Ok, Mr. Bernardo, I want you to take a look at the body and tell me if you knew this woman."

The dean blinked twice and swallowed once.

"No need, no need. It's Mildred; Professor Mildred Stark, a member of the faculty, and a—"

Chan interjected.

"Pardon, please, but I must interrupt to compliment very experienced academic sage for remarkable eyesight— capable of identifying body from across room, without seeing its face."

"Well?" Buckley demanded. "What about it? You been in this room before?"

"I—I can tell it's Professor Stark—because the hair is gray, and—and—"

"And?"

"Her—her shoes—I can see those, and she is, er, was fond of . . . remarkable footwear," he concluded lamely.

"You look at women's feet a lot?" Buckley inquired. "Or just hers? Maybe you knew her outside the classroom, so to speak?"

A bit of Bernardo's normal manner surfaced, and his tone recalled many long-past admonishments of disrespectful undergraduates.

"Sirrah, I resent your implication. The very idea—this university is a place of the highest ethical standards, and your insinuation is insulting."

"And do your university ethics cover the occasional dead body showing up? Because if not," Buckley paused, "I'd like a better answer to my question. Let me try again— let's say you didn't know this Stark woman that way, but you knew her shoes?"

The dean was deflated, and his careworn face reddened. "As it happens, I have made a study of footwear, especially the shodding of females in history unto the current day"—his glare invited any contradiction of what followed—"for purely academic purposes. The other women on this campus, faculty, students, others, without exception, disport themselves in commonplace style. Purely pedestrian, in more than one sense of the word."

"Fine, we'll qualify you as the campus shoe expert," Buckley made a dismissive gesture as the dean appeared ready to debate the appropriateness of such a characterization. His train of thought was derailed briefly by the almost wraithlike departure of the fingerprint expert, who nodded in Buckley's general direction and slipped silently from the room. The detective returned to the dean. "Let's move on. Tell me what you know about Mildred Stark, and what she might have been doing in this room. In that order, please."

"Without reviewing her entire *curriculum vitae* . . . her résumé, her history here and elsewhere," he added hastily, realizing that even minimal Latin—not to mention Greek—would be of little use in the present situation. "I can tell you, in brief, that she has been a valued member of the faculty here for two, perhaps three years. The provost's office would, of course, have more exact details of her employment history. Dedicated to her research, her students—a very serious person indeed.

"As for what she was doing in this room, I could not begin to speculate. As you have, no doubt, concluded already, it is used mainly for storage and, to the best of my knowledge of such things, is kept locked. Not that there's anything of monetary value, excepting the ceremonial mace; it has, certainly, historical value to our institution. But otherwise, academic robes are kept here, the diploma covers and other annual ephemera of academic ceremonies, also."

Buckley flipped through his brief notes and decided he had enough for the moment. "I guess that does it for now. Unless—" he remembered his manners, and his unofficial colleague. "Unless Mr. Chan has any questions?"

"Thank you; only one, please." Chan bowed slightly to the dean, out of respect for an elder. "Can you, perhaps, describe this woman as a person—did she have friends, or were there some who disliked her?"

The dean considered for a moment. "I'm hardly aware of all the faculty's practice of collegiality. Or lack thereof, but—there's always talk, of course. I would say that she had difficulty dealing with a great many colleagues. Bernardo's lips pursed. "She had . . . shall we say, a strong personality."

"Excuse the interruption please—you say 'many' colleagues. But not all found her distasteful?"

"Some, perhaps many, but not all. You see, Mr. Chan" —the dean's tone shifted to lecture mode, instructive and only faintly pompous—"she was beyond the ken of most of her students because of the complexity and aggressive nature of her views on practically all subjects. Especially international politics, the appalling situation in some parts of the world today. Ergo, the same attitude, the same opinions, that many of her faculty colleagues—how many, I'm sure I don't know—found off-putting seemed to endear her to a small number."

"Names of these like-minded ones, please?"
Bernardo's lips toward the faintest imitation of a smile. "Our *Sancta Trinitas*."

Buckley interjected. "Come again?"

"I beg your pardon. The three who come to mind

immediately have been given the jocular sobriquet of the Holy Trinity. Although," he frowned, "there's nothing divine or devout about them. I prefer to think of them as the three musketeers."

"Ok," The detective sighed. He was not interested in theology, Latin, or French adventure novels. "But their real names, please?"

"Hmm? Oh, I beg your pardon. Eduardo Dimayuga, our man of chemistry; the young French scholar, Jacques Marc. And, oh, that fellow Silva."

CHAPTER VIII

"SO MANY QUESTIONS ALL AT ONCE"

Buckley and Chan exchanged a glance at this additional tidbit concerning the uncooperative Professor Silva. Both silently wished that he could be recalled without delay, but—thought Buckley—time enough to question him later. Chan exchanged courtesies with Bernardo, who exited to make way for a seething provost. Merriweather had informed Gertrude Winget that he could wait no longer; she and Rose Chan remained in the classroom down the hall with Mallory.

"Gentlemen—my time is valuable, and I wish to offer you every possible aid." His demeanor assumed command of the meeting. "Acting for the president in his absence, I cannot delay any longer, waiting for you to question others—first the library, now this, I have much to attend to."

His pause for breath allowed Buckley to resume control of the interview.

"I'm sure that Mr. Chan agrees with me, we respect your position, Mr.—uh, Provost Merriweather. And we just ask that you respect ours, and cooperate to the best of your ability."

"Of course, of course. How can I assist?"

"For the record, then—did you know the deceased?"

Buckley's gesture lacked grace, but the point was clear. "And, if so, how well did you know her?"

Glancing toward the body, Merriweather cleared his throat before replying.

"You're speaking of Professor Stark, a member of the faculty. A fine researcher. She's been with us for several years. To be precise, I believe that this is—that is, was—her third academic year here." He paused. "This is unprecedented, dreadful. And for the president to be absent, the board—"

"Yeah, we wish the president was here, too," Buckley interrupted. "But you—you're the head academic, the chief of the faculty, right? How well did you know this woman—professionally, personally . . . ?"

The provost locked eyes with the detective, his mouth in a thin line.

"Not at all well. Professionally, I have limited individual interaction with faculty—that role is the dean's." His eyes narrowed. "Personally, I knew nothing of her."

Chan, deep in thought, roused himself.

"Pardon this interruption, but deceased woman had been here almost three years. Yet you knew her not at all?"

"Not at all." Merriweather's hands, in his lap, became fists. "The academic affairs of a university, even a small one such as this, are extraordinarily complex and time-consuming. Ranking second to the president, I find myself engaged in matters that require—that demand—a certain . . . detachment. And," he added, "I have no time for small talk, idle chatter, that sort of thing."

He rose.

"And this questioning has now become just that. I did not know Professor Stark. I am sorry she is dead, and I wish you well in your investigation. I, for one, believe that the most thorough examination of this situation should be completely transparent. Any wrongdoing must be exposed, publicized and corrected so that we preserve the confidence that our donors, our students and their parents have placed in this institution."

Buckley shrugged.

"You can go, but I'm sure we'll be speaking again. This is an ongoing investigation, and no one is above suspicion. I'm sure you appreciate—"

But Merriweather was already out the door.

Chan grinned. "Academic world is strange place, I think. Perhaps he has something to hide?"

"Everyone does, Mr. Chan, you know that. Especially in the case of homicide, if it is homicide."

"I think Rose Chan is next," Buckley continued, after consulting his notes. "You want to start the questions, Mr. Chan? She's your daughter, after all."

"Your kind consideration is appreciated, but I prefer we observe proper police procedure. I will, of course," Chan said with an almost straight face, "hover in background, asserting parental authority if necessary. This young woman, in my experience, not always cooperative."

Buckley laughed. "I get you—I'm a father myself. Ok, it's your call. I'll start, and if she gets feisty she's all yours."

Rose Chan entered the room, Buckley gestured to a chair and she sat, composed, hands folded in her lap.

"Now, Miss Chan, I think we can skip the introductions," Buckley began. "Your father is helping me sort things out, and he's going to stay here while we have our talk, but remember that this is a serious business." He pointed toward the body, and Rose turned to look at it, shuddered and averted her gaze. "Can you identify the victim? Somebody you knew or had seen around campus, maybe?"

Rose nodded. "I can't see her face, but I'm pretty sure it's Professor Stark. Her hair—it's short, not bobbed, not in a bun—and then, of course," she smiled. "There are the shoes. She was known for them, I guess."

"You work in the provost's office, right?" Rose nodded. "Did you see her there, or somewhere else, or have any opportunity to see her, get to know her?"

"So many questions all at once," Rose pointed out. "I'll do my best. First, I do work in the provost's office, part-time. I can't be there all the time, because I'm also a law school student here. Number two: Faculty are in and out of the office, and I don't always see them come and go—so she may have been there for one or more meetings, but I can't be sure. Three: Did I ever see her 'somewhere else.' You have to remember"—deference to authority vanished—"that a young Chinese woman, even a 'good' Chinese woman, an American who works at a university, just doesn't move in the same social circles as a professor." She avoided her father's gaze and looked defiantly at Buckley.

"Please"—Chan spoke quickly before Buckley could respond—"Detective Buckley is not responsible for American views of Chinese people, negative or positive. Better to reserve indignation for more appropriate setting."

"Sorry, Dad. And Mr. Buckley." She turned a wry face to the detective. "I guess I forgot for a second why we're here. It's just that the odds of me running into any faculty member—especially a hotshot who wears snazzy shoes—in Chinatown are, well, pretty slim."

"Translation, please, of unfortunate American slang words used by expensively educated daughter—at least for older Chinese. Maybe Detective Buckley knows vocabulary of youth, but I do not." Buckley started to react, thought better of it, and rubbed his face to conceal a smile.

"Sorry, Dad," Rose grinned, even in the face of parental chiding. "I guess saying she thought she and her shoes were the bee's knees doesn't help? Ok, ok." Her father had started to speak, but Rose saw what was coming and continued. "The word on her was that she had a high opinion of herself, at least when it came to fashion, and her shoes were just, I suppose, evidence of that. Who wears evening shoes all day long?

"Oh, but this might be helpful. People said that she was acquainted with some younger members of the faculty, socially, and that they were men." Rose reflected. "And if that's true, it must've been some kind of intellectual relationship. Most of the unattached 'junior faculty' as they call them would be looking for more of a real dish than, well, Professor Stark."

"Hmm. Well, we're not interested in any high-toned debates she was having, or the dating habits of the rest of the faculty," Buckley said dismissively. "It seems fair to say you knew her slightly, and you have no idea why someone might want to see her out of the way—or do you?"

Rose shrugged. "I just can't imagine why anyone would want to do something"—she glanced toward the body and quickly looked away—"so brutal."

Buckley nodded. "Right. We'll leave it at that, for now. But if you think of anything that might help, if something happens in your work that jogs your memory . . .you'll let us know." It was not a question.

"Just a suggestion—you should talk to Castor and Pollux." Seeing the detectives' blank expressions, she elaborated. "Sorry—their names are Caspar and Paul Poovey, but everybody calls them Castor and Pollux. Two old men who clean the buildings, do odd jobs—maintenance work."

"Why do you think they would know something about this?" Buckley scratched his ear absent-mindedly with his pencil.

"It's nothing in particular," Rose hastened to explain. "They just come and go, from building to building, and they have a kind of gossipy reputation. Everybody jokes that they seem to know things almost before they happen."

"Poovey, Caspar and Paul." McCaffrey made a note of the names. "Mr. Chan, anything you'd like to ask before we move on?"

"Nothing at this time, thank you." He addressed Rose. "Perhaps daughter and cousin still wish to meet at café you mentioned, maybe one hour from now?"

"Sure. It's Locus Bonum, just two blocks from here, and don't keep us waiting—we have lots to discuss," Rose said, and departed to make way for the next interview subject.

As though responding to a cue, Gertrude Winget knocked sharply on the half-open door.

"I assume you're ready for me? That is—I was the last in the room, and I thought—"

"Come right in, Miss . . ." Buckley glanced at his notes, and Chan supplied the name.

"This lady, Gertrude Winget, and I became acquainted in provost's office where she works."

Buckley closed the door and gestured toward a chair. Sinking into the seat, the woman clasped a handkerchief and looked from one detective to the other.

"Now, then, Miss Winget. I apologize for saving you till last, but I'm hoping that you can shed some light on this situation. Why don't you tell us—"

"But I don't know anything," Winget interjected. "I just went into the room to look for something—it's used mostly for storage—and found the . . . body."

"SO MANY QUESTIONS ALL AT ONCE"   81

Chan looked up sharply as Winget's voice trailed off. The detective thought she looked puzzled, as though something unexpected had occurred to her.

"So, you went to look for what, exactly?" Buckley's pencil paused over the official notepad.

"It's not important—the academic regalia for ceremonies is stored there, and a question was asked during a committee meeting yesterday," she stopped. "What does it matter? I went into the room, I found her, I was frightened. I think I screamed."

"That you did, from what I've been told," said Buckley. "And you didn't touch anything?"

"Nothing." The response was firm. "And I don't see why—"

"One moment, please." Chan raised his hand. "This room, is it kept locked—some of what is stored here has value?"

"Not for the average person, there's no money kept here—no valuables," Winget replied. "The ceremonial items, the regalia and mace and all those things—they would be expensive to replace, but of no practical value. And, yes," she added, almost as an afterthought, "the room is normally locked. I have a key."

"Was it locked when you went there?" Buckley demanded.

"I'm not sure," she frowned. "Let me recall—I was hurrying and tried the knob first, in a terrible rush, you know, and . . . " She stopped and considered. "It was unlocked. I'm sure of it."

"And I'm guessing that yours isn't the only key to this room," Buckley sighed. "Who else has one?"

"Mine is the key most often used," the woman replied with authority. "The room and its contents are the responsibility of the provost's office, and the key is kept in my middle desk drawer. Which is . . . never locked," she concluded regretfully.

"What about the maintenance people, the cleaning crew, the—"

"Oh, I suppose some of those staff may have a key, but really," she looked Buckley full in the face. "We're not the kind of place that locks everything up tightly all of the time, you know. This is a university, an academic community. We trust each other."

"Well, sister—er, Miss Winget," the exasperated detective replied. "That's all well and good, but it's pretty clear that somebody with a key must've unlocked that door. And that means your colleague's death was anything but an accident. Hell's bells—this was no accident!"

"You mean—"

Chan nodded. "Unlocked door just one more strong indication, and I fear coroner's report will confirm the word that Detective Buckley is too polite to use."

"Murder."

CHAPTER IX

SILENCE IN THE STACKS

Winget departed, and an officer standing guard outside the "murder room," as Buckley had dubbed it, entered and handed him a note from the fingerprint expert, who had left the room some time ago.

"Fingerprint man has come and gone, and his note says, surprise, there are prints. Lots of prints. Mostly smudged. Dead woman's prints are not on the mace, as far as he could tell, and as for that book you asked about—"

Chan's eyebrows lifted.

"—only smudges, I'm afraid."

"Now that fingerprint expert has finished his work, I am happy to assist in examining contents of the room," Chan replied. "And, with your permission, I will borrow that one small book—maybe for bedtime reading."

"You think it means something?"

Chan shrugged. "Tiny book may be big clue—or wild goose. Perhaps digesting contents will suggest possibilities."

"Suit yourself, then. The boys have looked over the room, but I want to see if they missed anything."

Buckley turned his attention to the bookcases that lined the room and their dusty contents. A motley array of old books, reference works mostly, framed certificates, statuettes, and curios from other colleges and universities crowded the lower shelves; the upper shelves were empty. The detective was unimpressed.

"This stuff looks like it hasn't been touched in months, maybe longer," he grunted. "A lot of dusty junk.

"And a whole library," he added, gesturing at the shelves and desk. "But I don't think our murderer was here to check out a book."

Chan nodded. "Little-used room suggests place for private meetings, maybe hasty conversation between two persons who wished to be alone."

Having pocketed the book, Chan ran a hand over the rack's dozens of robes and examined his fingers.

"Unlike dusty shelves, this college clothing seems new to room," he told Buckley. "Maybe people come and go to this room from time to time—not for books, but to select robe?"

"We'll ask that what's-her-name, Winget," Buckley said. "Anyway, what if they do? These professors are a different breed, but they don't fight over the latest gown and club each other, do they? And what about that explosion, Mr. Chan, how does that tie in? Can't be a coincidence."

"Sometimes coincidence causes even suspicious events," Chan replied, "but we do not know yet what led to library fire and smoke. In this room I think circumstances are like old Chinese saying about man who pretends to be tiger—but inside is only a sheep."

"Come again?"

"Body of unfortunate woman in locked room is impressive event, and we are maybe quick to assume it relates to other things, that it is part of some larger purpose." Chan looked around the room. "My connection with this case is unofficial, but I would say to you, walk slowly on this path."

"I appreciate the advice, Mr. Chan, but for now my money's on a connection of some kind. And as for this room, I'm done here if you are."

"Finished, except to call two things to your attention." He pointed to the long rug. "Smudges and marks on rug, some over blood stains, indicate one or more persons in room after vital liquid stained area around body." He walked a few steps toward the body and pointed to the face of the corpse. "Second item, observe blood stain on cheek—smeared appearance suggests some contact with face of deceased by some person. Both these small indications worth considering carefully."

Buckley frowned. "You think more than one other person was present?"

"Possible," Chan said, "but too early to make big conclusions from small clues. Perhaps college cleaners mentioned by daughter Rose may be able to add to our knowledge of comings and goings. Strange that two persons with reputation for being everywhere at college are not close at hand when event of importance is unfolding." He smiled. "As for investigation, my humble brainpower added to your knowledge and experience will eventually reveal truth of matter."

"Two brains are better than one, you mean?" Buckley chuckled. "Let's hope so." They left the room, and Buckley made arrangements with the officer in the hall to have the body removed.

"With your permission, I will depart to keep appointment with daughter Rose." Chan bowed slightly. "Please oblige me by calling Chancellor Hotel, Powell Street, if developments occur. Regret fills me since I have done nothing of note to assist you, but maybe you will need no help from visiting parent to reach quick solution."

Buckley promised to keep him informed, and Chan departed the campus in search of Locus Bonum.

"OK, Dad—spill the beans. What's going on?"

Rose took no time for social niceties once the two had settled into a corner booth and ordered tea—green with lemon—from a uniformed waitress.

"Thank you for adding 'bean-spilling' to your father's growing vocabulary of American slang expressions," Chan returned with a smile. "And social custom demands that I inquire of you as to your health and experience of the day—I trust that you are well and enjoying life experiences appropriate to youth? Also, where is your cousin who was to join us?"

Rose laughed.

"I'm fine, and she's studying. Said to pay her respects to you." Rose clasped her hands and offered a traditional, albeit mischievous, bow. "Now—put me in the picture. Have you solved the case? Or is there more than one? What's the deal?"

"Please!" Chan grimaced in mock disapproval. "Avalanche of slang threatens to bury hiker in wilderness of American language. To answer questions shortly, I would say: 'No. Perhaps. Not sure.'"

He paused as the waitress arrived with a pot of tea and two cups. Pouring for both of them, Chan took a sip of the steaming liquid and continued.

"Speaking more fully, not much time has passed since your parent arrived to pursue investigation of, maybe, simple financial questions. Then, trouble at college library—"

"People are saying it was a bomb," Rose interrupted. "and cousin Rose has a special friend who's a policeman, and he says the same."

"I had suspected as much. And to these two circumstances we add body in room. Still, I would answer, 'perhaps,' to question of one case, or several."

Rose grinned.

"Even a beginning law student knows you can't answer an either-or question with 'perhaps.' Anyway, nothing happens at a sleepy little college for years, and then three out-of-the-ordinary events—"

"Investigation will reveal whether all three are members of same family, unrelated, or . . . "

"Or?"

"Maybe events are acquainted with each other in some way we cannot yet understand."

Chan picked up their bill, and a small piece of paper under it fluttered to the floor. Scooping it up, Rose read aloud its brief message scrawled in pencil.

"'Spend more time with your daughter. Then go home. Justice must be done.'" Her brow wrinkled. "Is this the latest fashion in sinister notes received by detectives?"

Chan examined the note, and stowed it carefully in a black leather wallet before replying.

"Someone wishes to direct my activities away from university happenings, and same person also suffers from need to mix specific instructions with grand statement."

"But justice for who or what?"

"Justice for 'whom,'" Chan corrected with a smile. "This much of English grammar I know."

"Ok, 'whom,' but you haven't spilled any beans about our investigation," Rose replied. "Tell me what you're thinking about the murder—it is murder, right?"

"First," Chan corrected, "not 'our' investigation. Second, possible suspects are many, because already I sense rivalries and longstanding divisions in learning community where acquiring knowledge, not engaging in conflict, should be priority. Third . . ."

The detective fell silent, as though struck by an aspect of the situation that had not occurred to him previously.

"Dad?"

Chan came to himself with a start.

"So sorry. Third point—police and coroner will confirm whether untimely death is murder. And I must clarify earlier point—*possible* suspects are many, but *probable* suspects not so many."

"You thought of something," Rose said accusingly. "What are you not telling me?"

Chan grinned. "Things I think of that I do not share are numerous, as many as drops of water swimming in bay of San Francisco."

He wagged a forefinger, a familiar fatherly gesture to Rose, and went on:

"Rest assured that all will be revealed in due course. Still we have much to discover about unfortunate woman—and other recent events at university."

The two Chans concluded their conversation with a summary of family doings at home. Leaving Rose to pursue her studies, Chan stopped at a telephone booth, leaving a regretful message with June Kirk's office. Much as he would like to renew old ties, the current investigation came first. He took a cab to Mission Police Station in search of Buckley. A uniformed officer directed him to an inner office where Buckley was on the telephone, seated behind a cluttered desk.

"Yeah, right, right. I heard you the first time," he snapped impatiently, interrupting the tinny speech streaming from the phone. "Just let me know if you get anything else on this."

Banging down the receiver, he shook his head and Chan's hand. "Experts. This one says 'inconclusive' sums up the official cause of the college library blast and fire. *Maybe* an incendiary device, *maybe* a timer-detonator, or *maybe* something simpler, like a long fuse and a stick of dynamite."

Chan nodded sympathetically.

"Certainty in police science almost as rare as chicken's visit to dentist," he said. "Sad to say, I bring you information that may add to already tangled situation."

Briefly he detailed his interest in probing the university's finances and pulled his wallet from an inner pocket, passing the note across the desk. Buckley scanned the message and looked up at Chan.

"Trouble seems to multiply in your general vicinity, Mr. Chan, and I can't help thinking that the university's questionable finances, a blown-up building and murder are connected in some way—even two of the three." Buckley scratched his head. "But for the life of me, I don't see how."

Chan shrugged.

"For now I can agree only that you have 'swell hunch,' as my American-educated children would call it, but I will continue to seek possible connections. Best if you pursue official lines of inquiry, and I fish in unofficial waters. Police have perhaps learned more about unfortunate woman, Mildred Stark, and her background?"

Buckley crossed the room to a water cooler, filled two paper cups, handed one to his guest and set the other on his desk. Pulling a manila folder from a stack, he passed it to Chan.

"Read for yourself, but I don't see anything that

suggests someone would want to kill the woman." Buckley ticked off Stark's résumé highlights on nicotine-stained fingers. "Mildred Louise Stark, age 62, native of New England. Never married. No immediate family—that we can find, anyway. College in Boston, then more degrees in New York, teaching job at a university in Philadelphia . . . "

"Woman achieved some success in city known for fraternal fondness," Chan noted, leafing through the papers. "Many years at Philadelphia university led to promotion, professor title."

He closed the folder and returned it to the desk.

"Why, then, come across country to small university here, from well-established career at prestigious Eastern institution? And make such a move at an age when end of successful career is in sight, and retirement beckons?"

Buckley snorted. "Sometimes I think too much education drains the common sense out of people. But more to the point, I'm interested in what she was doing in that room—not so much why she moved to our fair city."

"Must consider presence of victim here as part of larger story," Chan said thoughtfully. "Maybe there is something about her that we do not yet know that will reveal connection to other person in room. Perhaps she left Philadelphia to escape trouble, which then followed her."

"Maybe, maybe," Buckley said dismissively. "Meanwhile, I need to nail down a few facts that point to an actual person. I can't take a 'maybe' case to the district attorney."

Chan rose and bowed slightly.

"I apologize for engaging in speculation, not helpful to official inquiry at this stage. Suggest that we each pursue avenue of investigation and compare results later?"

"Fine, fine." Buckley nodded. "You understand where

I'm coming from, don't you, Mr. Chan? I'm grateful for your help, but this situation with the university—a lot of important people in this city are talking, and I'm under a lot of pressure." He glanced at his watch, noting the lateness of the hour.

Chan grinned. "No offense taken by me. I am all too familiar with noise from all quarters that accompanies high-profile case.

"And maybe," he added as he opened the door, "Some of those many in city who are talking will say something that points the way to truth."

The next morning, John Quincy Winterslip climbed the university library stairs to the third floor, silently echoing Charlie Chan's parting words to Buckley the evening before. *Sooner or later*, he thought, *someone is going to talk too much—to me, or to the proper authorities. Maybe this will be the start.*

Making his way through the stacks, row after row of towering shelves packed with books, he arrived in a little-used, somewhat dusty philosophy section. The telephone message Winterslip had received specified the topic ("your inquiry"), time and location, and the anonymous caller had stressed confidentiality. *A bit too cloak-and-dagger,* Winterslip had thought, but he felt obligated to keep the appointment.

He was a few minutes early, and silence was his only companion in the appointed place. Light was scarce in this section of the stacks, and Winterslip could not see through the row of books to the other side where, he assumed, his anonymous caller would make himself or herself known.

After a brief period that seemed much longer, he heard a slight noise from the expected location. "Hello?"

Winterslip whispered through the shelves. "I believe you phoned my office?

Silence.

The young man persisted. "Thanks for meeting me here," he whispered to the unseen one. "You know that I'm interested in the university's financial situation—in possible wrongdoing—and your message said that you have information for me?"

A rustling of paper and shuffling of books was his only reply. Slowly, a bulky file folder made its way through the stack, squeezed between the tops of old books and the bottom of the shelf above.

"Here," a hoarse whisper replied as the folder made its way into Winterslip's waiting hands. He opened and quickly scanned the first few pages, paragraphs of narrative punctuated by rows of numbers.

"Where did you get this? Who are you?" Winterslip demanded, sotto voce.

Silence.

"Hello? Are you there?" This, in a louder voice, prompted an immediate rebuke from a passing librarian. "Sorry!" Winterslip whispered to her receding form.

Grasping the file folder, he quickly made his way around the stack to where his informant must have stood, but no one was there. He walked quickly through the library, all the way to the main entrance, and saw no one who appeared out of place. But he saw only a few students, deep in study, two custodians sweeping the main reading room, and staff reshelving books and restoring order disrupted by the recent intrusion of smoke, the odor of which still lingered. It was the same story outside; he could see no guilty-looking party who appeared to have just surreptitiously delivered confidential information.

Winterslip shrugged. *The "who" in this case is not as important as the "what," as in the contents of the folder,* he thought. Time enough to determine who the informant was later on.

His immediate goal was to share this windfall with someone who could unravel its riddle.

CHAPTER X

LUNCH WITH MISS WINGET

"You have made diligent efforts, and this potential treasure trove is the result—first possible evidence of money troubles earlier described without details by our friend the dean," Charlie Chan told his once-again junior detection partner.

Winterslip had phoned Chan's hotel, and the two had retreated to cousin Roger's conference room for a private conversation. The younger man responded modestly, shrugging in mock rebuttal.

"All in a day's work, and very little was required of me—just a trip to the library," he said with a grin. "Do you think someone at the university is on our side?"

"That question, among others, remains to be answered," Chan replied. "My humble examination of these papers convinces me that expert review is needed to reveal whether we have here real evidence of wrongdoing. Or maybe we only pursue untamed water fowl."

Winterslip laughed.

"You can't fool me, Charlie. I've known you long enough to be sure that you are perfectly familiar with the term, 'wild goose chase.' Anyway, whether the goose is wild, or the chase itself, I think some of the answers we're looking for are in this little stack of papers."

A knock at the door was followed by the entrance of a conservatively clad young-looking woman with a quizzical expression.

"You wanted to see me, Mr. Winterslip?"

"Grace, please come in and meet my friend Charlie Chan." Winterslip and the detective stood as introductions were performed.

"Don't be fooled by youthful appearances, Charlie. Grace Carson is our number one financial analyst." Winterslip smiled. "If these papers have a story to tell, she'll find it in no time."

"I'm pleased to meet you, Mr. Chan, and I must tell you how much I've enjoyed reading about you in the papers over the years." Grace Carson shook the detective's hand with a firm grip, her professional expression relaxing briefly. "I never thought I'd be meeting you in person."

Chan bowed in acknowledgement, noting the woman's no-nonsense demeanor and keen eye.

"I am happy to make acquaintance of 'number one financial analyst' from whom we seek answers to tangled money questions," Chan turned inquisitively to Winterslip. "Am I correct in assumption that we can disclose all concerning this matter to Miss Carson? As my daughter has said it, 'spill beans?'"

"That's right, Charlie," Winterslip laughed. "Spill away." Handing the sheaf of papers to Carson, Chan briefly described the fiscal concerns that had brought him to the city, omitting the other events on campus. The analyst listened intently, glancing at the documents.

"To be clear, then, gentlemen," she said crisply, when Chan had concluded. "You want me to make more than a cursory examination of these records to determine whether irregularities are present, and whether any such irregularities arise from simple incompetence, negligence or, potentially, some criminal intent. Have I stated the matter accurately?"

Winterslip grinned in Chan's direction. "What did I tell you Charlie? Isn't she the answer to our prayers—or as Rose would say, 'the cat's whiskers'?" Turning to his staff member, Winterslip responded to her summary.

"You've said it better than I could have, Grace, and I would only ask that you make this task a priority. Anything else you're working on at the moment—please ask Walter to take it over. Charlie, anything to add?"

"Only gratitude to both of you for prompt attention to this matter," Chan responded with a smile.

With the mysterious folder in hand, Grace Carson nodded and departed.

"She's been with the firm five years, and I tell you, Charlie, she has more brains than accountants with far more experience," Winterslip lit a cigarette and crossed his legs. "While she's looking things over, what can I do to help move things along? Cousin Roger will no doubt be asking me for a report soon."

"First things first," Chan declared, with a slight twinkle in his eyes. "Am I correct in assuming that measure of woman's competence compares favorably with facial hair of feline animal?"

Winterslip laughed.

"Cut it out, Charlie. Rose has told me you know more American slang than you let on. But seriously," he continued. "What more can we do right now? My conversation with the president didn't result in anything except pleasantries. And our friend the dean has nothing but suspicions to go on."

"I suggest you cultivate conversation with purposeful woman who may know more about inner workings of university offices than even men at top of administrative heap—"

"Rose?" the younger man interjected. "She's only been working there for a short—"

"Please!" Chan interrupted with one eyebrow raised. "I refer to redoubtable Miss Winget: brisk, efficient. She may have much to tell, given extended opportunity to converse with handsome, successful professional man."

"Who, me?"

Chan smiled.

"I'm sure I don't know why you're so kind as to invite me to lunch, unless it's to 'pump me'—as the undergraduates say, and such an indelicate expression—for gossip," said Gertrude Winget.

She and Winterslip were seated at a corner table in a quiet restaurant some distance from the university. He had convinced her to partake of a modest wine—"in thanks for your dedication to duty, and for taking the time to speak with me"—which she sipped tentatively.

"Why, Miss Winget! Nothing could be further from my thoughts," Winterslip replied, with only a trace of mock indignation. "The truth is, when I asked my cousin Roger for the name of a person best suited to explain to me the complexities of such a great institution, the first and only name he recommended to me was—"

"Mr. Winterslip, the trustee, said that?" She took a third sip of wine. "Good heavens! Members of the board never acknowledge staff, and I had no idea . . ."

The younger Winterslip silently absolved himself from constructing the fictional recommendation, making a mental note to prepare Roger for any future remarks the board member might receive from his new fan.

"That's fine, then." He continued. "What I want to know about the university's innerworkings begins with a better understanding of the people, you see. Because dedicated people—such as you—are really the makings of any organization. And you work with such interesting people—"

"Indeed, indeed," she agreed. A fourth sip emptied her glass, which Winterslip refilled—not neglecting his own. "I can tell you, young man, that the intellectual talent at the university really beggars description. Amazing, truly.

"But at the same time," she paused as a waitress deposited a first course before them. "At the same time, these brilliant men—and, sadly, they are mostly men—are quite human."

Winterslip sensed an opening.

"Quite so, brilliant but human. But tell me, in what way do their more ordinary qualities come to light? Are there friendships? Rivalries?"

Winget nodded archly.

"One could write a book. It's shocking, but sometimes those more experienced in life, despite their intellectual attainments, behave just as badly as the greenest undergraduates. Worse, even."

"Surely you don't mean respectable figures like Dean Bernardo?"

"Heavens, no!" She laughed immoderately, holding the cloth napkin to her lips to muffle the unseemly mirth. "That man's a cross between a saint and a worried old woman. No, no, apart from his interest in women's footwear—an odd research interest, that—the dean does not exhibit any of the earthier human qualities.

"Now, the provost," she continued. "He's far more, *human,* I would say. Frustrated, ambitious—"

"Really? What about?"

Winget laughed, more moderately this time. "What every academic administrator seems to dream of, of course! Being president."

Winterslip refilled her glass, and his, a second time; another bottle had arrived with their lunch entrées.

"President of . . .?"

"A university, of course," she responded tartly. "Unfamiliar as you are with *The Academy* (Winterslip knew without a doubt that she had reverently capitalized the words), you don't know that all of them—the men, I mean—simply *yearn* to be president of a university. Either the one at which they currently work, or one which they will eventually seek out.

"President Emerson himself is another example," she continued. "He spent most of his career in calculated fashion, seizing every opportunity to build a curriculum vitae that supported presidential aspirations. And it must have worked."

"But everyone can't be a college president," Winterslip said. "What happens to all the runners-up, the disappointed candidates for the top job?"

"Look no further than the example I just cited. The provost could have been president here, and he might still be president of some other institution. Or he could—"

"Could what?"

Winget took something between a sip and a gulp before answering.

"I was just going to say that the provost could still be president here, if anything were to happen to President Emerson. Something unexpected. In such a case, it would be quite likely for the board to appoint him to the presidency, at least temporarily. Perhaps permanently."

Winterslip let the silence hang for several seconds, hoping for more from his slightly tipsy luncheon partner. But he was disappointed.

"Now, if you'll excuse me," said Winget, placing her napkin neatly on the table, "I really must be going—the provost's office must not remain untended for long. Thank you for an excellent lunch."

Winterslip rose, shook the proffered hand, and resumed his seat as Winget departed, weaving her way through the maze of occupied tables. He lit a cigarette and frowned in concentration.

Does she know more than she's letting on—or less? He summed up: This is a maiden lady whose main interest in life is the place where she has worked for many years and seems to know a lot about her fellow administrators. And the faculty, too. *I think I've only scratched the surface, but who knows*, he thought.

This kind of speculation is better left to Chan and the proper authorities, Winterslip concluded. *But,* he told himself, *I can give him the benefit of my personal observations when I report on lunch with the lady.* When one comes down to it, he mused, the university is like a little town where some people seem to know everyone else's business.

President Emerson made his way across the university campus, briefcase in hand. First stop, the provost's office where he strode past the vacant secretarial desk and tapped on the inner office door before entering.

"Christopher!" Merriweather rose from behind his desk where stacks of papers and several opened volumes, a ponderous collection, demonstrated a devotion to matters of great import. "Welcome back. I have much to tell you"

"I've heard a great deal already," Emerson replied with a

sigh. "But you might as well begin from the beginning and fill in any gaps in my knowledge of recent events."

The provost complied, starting with the explosion at the library and moving on to the finding of the body and the police investigation into both events. It was a brisk and efficient summary.

"That poor woman," Emerson said abstractedly. "And the police—what are they saying? Do they know who was responsible for these things?"

"The detective in charge of both incidents believes them to be connected," Merriweather replied. "He is, perhaps," the provost added drily, "not the most astute practitioner of his trade."

The president gazed out the window for a few seconds, then turned toward Merriweather.

"And you—you've had the opportunity to observe their aftermath, if not the events themselves—do you believe the same person is responsible for both?"

"Impossible." The provost tut-tutted. "What does a bomb or a fire or whatever it was in the library have to do with a faculty death?"

"Hmm. Ultimately all this is for the police to determine, of course." Emerson nodded. "I'm sure you acted as you thought best in my absence, and I thank you.

"Now," he said, gesturing toward the papers on the provost's desk. "We cannot ignore more mundane matters—the end of the semester is almost upon us. And that means commencement.

"As president," he declared, pronouncing his title with more than a hint of self-importance, "I will address the candidates for graduation and the entire university community at the close of the ceremony. My remarks." He handed a folder to the provost. "I would be interested in your thoughts on them."

"Of course," Merriweather replied, inwardly disgusted. His face unchanged, the provost's inner voice was outraged: *How can this pompous windbag dismiss a colleague's death in such cavalier fashion—to talk about his idiotic speech?* he thought.

"Gentlemen, please pardon this unseemly interruption," a voice broke in. Startled by the unexpected visitor, president and provost looked up to see Charlie Chan in the doorway.

"Sorry to intrude unannounced," Chan continued, taking a few steps into the room, nodding toward the two surprised academics. "But no guardian of academic office present at desk outside."

"That's quite all right, Mr. Chan," Merriweather responded. "This is the president of the university, Dr. Emerson."

The president extended a hand, smiling stiffly. "Christopher Emerson, Mr. Chan. Your reputation precedes you, of course. How can we help you?" The three took seats as Chan replied.

"Seeking moment of provost's time, I heard two voices and now am hoping for opportunity to pose questions to both of you," he said. "More convenient to discuss recent events with both highest-ranking university officials at the same time—to eliminate unnecessary confusion."

"You are, then, working with the police?" Emerson asked. "I had been told that Detective . . ."

"Buckley," Merriweather provided promptly. "He's the detective in charge."

"Quite correct," Chan said. "As visitor to campus, I am here only in unofficial capacity. Still," he glanced at each of the men in turn, "Detective Buckley has welcomed my assistance, and words with both of you may provide his investigation with valuable assistance."

Chan's tone was deferential, but the point was clear. Emerson cleared his throat.

"Ask your questions, then. I'm sure we'll be happy to give you whatever assistance we can. As for me, I know little of the professor's death and the circumstances leading up to it as I was away at the time."

"Away where, please?"

"Two glorious days at the State Capitol and two magical nights at the Hotel Senator in Sacramento," Emerson said wryly. "Lobbying, Mr. Chan, is one of the less glamorous but necessary duties of a university president."

"And you returned to the campus when?"

"Just now. That is, I returned home this morning and came to campus within the last hour."

Chan nodded, turning to the provost.

"As for my whereabouts, I think you'll recall, Mr. Chan, that you and I were outside the library in the aftermath of the unfortunate incident there," Merriweather noted. "And that we adjourned to the conference room in this building a short time later. We were there when—"

"Thank you, yes," Chan interjected. "Excuse my rude interruption, but where were you before disturbance at library?"

"In my office," the provost said without hesitation. "The sound could be heard even there; the strangeness of the noise attracted my attention, and I went immediately to the scene.

"By the way, Mr. Chan," Merriweather continued. "Have the police come to any conclusion as to the nature of the library explosion?"

"Matter still under intense official investigation," Chan

replied blandly. He turned back to the president.

"You, perhaps, knew the unfortunate woman, Mildred Stark?"

"Only by name, I'm afraid," Emerson said. "My duties don't allow me to get to know all of the faculty well, and I usually leave the mentoring and management of them to the dean—and to the provost, of course," he nodded toward Merriweather.

"And you, perhaps, knew Professor Stark?" Chan's gaze rested upon the provost.

"I think I told you and Detective Buckley earlier that she was a respected researcher," Merriweather said pompously, "but did I know her personally? No."

Eduardo Dimayuga, professor of chemistry, was a worried man. Deep in the evaluation of student projects in a brightly lit laboratory (made possible by a wealthy alumnus), he scribbled notes on a freshly graded final exam and handed it to one of two remaining students in the room.

"Thanks, professor!" She smiled, gathered up her books and joined her apparent beau; Dimayuga nodded absently. *She deserves better than that musclebound oaf,* Dimayuga mused. The couple headed toward the door. *She will make a fine research chemist someday,* he thought, *if marriage and children—and the oaf—allow it.*

Finished with the final exam, Dimayuga locked the laboratory door behind him and headed toward his office down the hall. Hearing a ringing telephone, he quickened his pace, unlocked the door in a single motion, and entered.

"Hello? Who calls?" he spoke into the instrument. "Ah, it is you. I have told you—I am done with the matter. You have achieved your purpose, yes? Then it is finished."

The voice on the other end of the wire was insistent.

"But I tell you," the chemist said, "I want no more of your—*paano po sasabihin?*—conspiring. Enough of this. I go to the police."

Silence.

"Hello? You hear me? You make threats, you make noise—I am finished with you."

The silence ended with a single sentence. Dimayuga's shaking hand banged the receiver into its cradle.

"Professor?" A student was in the office doorway. "I was wondering if I might—"

"Not now!" Dimayuga shouted the words, then lowered his voice to a normal pitch. "Come back later, I cannot speak with you now—there is an important call I must make."

The student retreated, and the professor picked up the phone and dialed.

"Connect me with the police."

CHAPTER XI
A GRIM SCENE

Charlie Chan exited the taxi, after enjoying something he had rarely experienced before: a warm, sunny day in San Francisco. Today's warmth had reminded him of home and family. Sighing, he thought of Punchbowl Hill as he entered the ornate building. The Winterslip offices normally hummed with activity, but it was evening, and only a few staff were still at work.

"Mr. Winterslip's in a meeting down the hall, but he said to make yourself comfortable," the secretary told Chan. "He won't be long."

She returned to the outer office, leaving the detective alone with his thoughts—which quickly turned to curiosity. One can learn a lot from what a professional person takes to the office, and during his previous visit Chan had noted the presence of several framed photographs. Now, he took a closer look, to satisfy his curiosity. What he saw tended to confirm his earlier speculations.

"Charlie! Sorry to keep you waiting." Winterslip arrived in a rush, waving a folder of documents just returned to him by Grace Carson, who was a few steps behind. "Grace got the goods!"

"Mr. Winterslip's enthusiasm exceeds my findings," the woman asserted. "But, in my professional opinion, a pattern of financial misfeasance—possibly rising to the level of malfeasance—is evident in the records provided for my review."

Chan nodded. "You are not able to determine evidence of criminal wrongdoing?"

"Correct," she replied. "For that, a forensic audit would be required, and from Mr. Winterslip's direction to me"— her glance was answered by an affirmative nod—"such an intrusive action is not possible if the current degree of confidentiality is to be maintained.

"My findings are summarized for you both," she continued. "At best, one or more persons has been very careless in the handling of monies entrusted to the institution from donors. In my experience, a situation of this complexity doesn't create itself. In short, I sense a guiding hand in the movement and concealment of certain sums."

Winterslip frowned. "No smoke without fire, so to speak?"

Carson nodded. "Precisely. Beyond that, I cannot venture with any certainty. But," she concluded, "there is a good deal of smoke."

Winterslip lit a cigarette, adding real fumes to the troubling metaphor. "Thank you, Grace. This is enormously helpful. Well, Charlie," he said as Grace Carson left the room. "Where does that leave us? What's our next step?"

Chan gestured toward the folder. "Expert confirms uneasy feelings shared by dean. The numbers tell part of the story, so now we must ask ourselves: Who has need of money from university? Who could have access to it? Is monetary gain the only motive for tampering with finances?"

"What do you mean—what other motive could there be aside from the almighty dollar?"

The detective shrugged. "'The man who learns but does not reflect will be perplexed,'" he quoted. "We have learned from your helpful expert of finance, and now we must reflect. Still, there is much that can be done to advance our learning further."

"What, for instance?"

"Perhaps you can continue and expand efforts to collect university gossip. Numbers from accountant tell us there is smoke, and further conversation may point to person or persons who strike matches to create same." Chan raised a forefinger for emphasis. "When people talk, even well-educated university people, sometimes they reveal more than intended. Young professional man with influential cousin may receive better 'education' from them than middle-aged detective seeking clues."

"I get it—you want me to expand my personal interest in whatever stories our university friends have to tell me?"

"Your hammer has found the nail's head," Chan nodded. "Invite talk of various matters, some related to our interest in university money, others not directly related. All such conversation, from both innocent and not-so-innocent, may be helpful. Some roosters crow whether sun comes up or not. All such activity, of course, as time permits."

"Well, let's hope some of these roosters know what they're crowing about," Winterslip said puckishly. "I'm sure Roger would like to reassure the dean that we're doing what we can to secure the barnyard."

Winterslip's secretary appeared in the doorway. "Excuse me—a Detective Buckley is on the line, asking for Mr. Chan."

Chan nodded. "Took liberty of leaving telephone number of this office with official investigator in case of new developments," he explained to his host.

"Take it here, Charlie." Winterslip gestured toward the instrument on his desk. Chan held the phone to his ear; he could hear an animated conversation on the other end.

"Inspector Chan speaking—hello?"

"Charlie? This is Buckley. I just got the call, and I want you at the scene right away."

"Scene of—?"

"I'm afraid we've got another body, another dead professor from the university."

"Address, please," Chan wrote rapidly on the desk's notepad. "Thank you for timely call—leaving now to join you there."

Hanging up, Chan tore the slip of paper from the pad and retrieved his hat, his expression impassive. But Winterslip had seen and heard enough to know.

"Bad news, Charlie?"

"Sudden death of yet another professor," he replied. "I am called to the scene by Detective Buckley."

"Good heavens! I'll get my hat and come with you—"

"Please." Chan raised one hand, his other on the doorknob. "New death provides opportunity for more direct means of investigation, and we must shift our efforts. Not so important that you speak with others at university now, and your work here may yield valuable results. I ask that you concentrate on financial puzzle that the worthy Grace has explored. Much more to be learned there, I think."

Winterslip nodded. "Whatever you say, Charlie. I'll let you know what else we uncover here."

The hour was late when Chan arrived at the scene, a picturesque spot within sight of the university campus. In addition to the police presence, a small knot of onlookers had gathered to observe a grim scene. Buckley broke off a conversation with a uniformed officer, turning to greet his unofficial colleague.

"Thanks for coming, Charlie. I figured you'd want to see this first-hand, just in case."

"'In case'—?"

"Well, in case there's a connection." Buckley scratched his head. "This part of town, the university itself, quietest place you can imagine since I was pounding a beat. Then a body on campus, followed by another body—and both of them professors, too—a stone's throw from the campus.

"And that thing you're looking into—the financial funny business—if these things don't all hook up somehow, then we have one helluva batch of coincidences."

Chan nodded.

"First appearances like cat at scene of spilled milk— point to obvious conclusion. But what of this latest sad event?"

Buckley led the detective to the edge of a rectangular pool of water surrounded by flagstones, with decorative benches at either end. The body, recently retrieved from the water, lay covered on a stretcher near a waiting ambulance.

"This pool"—Buckley gestured toward the dark water—"the university people call it the 'reflecting pool.' It's at the edge of the campus property. Supposed to be a place where students and the professors can come to sit and . . ."

"Reflect?" Chan suggested.

"Yeah," Buckley replied grimly. "But it looks like this Professor Whatsis—Dimayuga 'reflected' a little too close to the water's edge. Or maybe someone was here to help him take a dip."

"Body show signs pointing to cause of death?"

Buckley grimaced. "It looks like accidental drowning, or maybe it's meant to look that way, the water's not that deep. He's got a bump on the temple, but he could have tripped and banged his head—with or without help. We'll have to wait for the medical examiner and coroner's reports.

"Meanwhile, what say we see who's curious enough to show up here, just to watch?" Buckley approached the dozen or so onlookers, looking for familiar faces. "Starting with these two." He approached a pair of grizzled men; Chan recalled Rose's description of "Castor and Pollux" Poovey: two old men who seem to know things almost before they happen. He had thought their earlier absence strange, and now here they were. Were they more than merely curious? Buckley had invited the two to "have a little chat." Moving away from poolside activity, he introduced Chan; Castor and Pollux nodded.

"People say you two know quite a lot about what goes on at the university," Buckley said without preamble. "Maybe you know something about this body in the pool— maybe you saw something, heard something—"

Pollux cleared his throat. "We were taking ourselves home from a wee jollification at the tavern—"

"Locus Bonum?" Buckley's notepad was put into service.

Pollux nodded. "We heard the commotion and came to see what all the fuss was about, and here we are."

Castor chimed in: "We thought it fair strange—all this noise, because earlier we heard—"

Pollux interrupted with a few well-chosen Welsh words. Their meaning was unclear to the two detectives, but Castor understood perfectly, and his mouth closed with a snap.

"What's the big idea?" Buckley was annoyed. "Hey, you,

whatever your name is—what did you say to him? And just what, exactly, did the two of you hear?"

"I told him to leave off borrowin' trouble," Pollux replied, with more than a trace of asperity. "In so many words, I said he should shut his big—"

"Yeah, I got that part," Buckley interjected. "What I want to know is, what was it that you heard?"

"Nothin' much," Pollux replied. "We had come away from the tavern, a few blocks, and we heard some shoutin', that's all."

Castor found his voice again. "It sounded like two fellas arguin'—but . . . "

"But what?" Buckley snapped. "Could you tell who it was—and what they were saying?"

"No." The two men replied with one voice. "Just a bit of back-and-forth," Pollux continued, "and then it stopped."

"Well, then—why were you so eager to shut his mouth?" Watkins pointed to the now-silent Castor.

"'Least said, soonest mended.,'" Pollux quoted. "That's what our ol' Grandda' used to say, and whatever we hear, on the job or off, we keep to ourselves."

"Perhaps," Charlie Chan interceded, "you would ignore vow of silence for good of university? Detective Buckley only wishes to shed light on recent events—two persons are dead, and any information you may possess about these happenings, or about explosion and fire at library—"

Pollux shook his head. "The only thing we know for certain about the library," he declared, "is the work that's still to be done to clear up the mess that was done by whoever did whatever it was that was done." Castor nodded in agreement as Pollux continued. "That work falls mostly to us, and as for tonight—we heard what I told you, no more."

Buckley snorted. "And what about the death of Professor Stark?"

"We know no more than you, and probably a great deal less," Pollux said firmly. "Idle talk and gossip—what good are they?"

"That's what we'd like to know," Buckley cried in exasperation. "Everything that you've heard and seen—anything that might have some bearing on—"

Chan raised his hand and interrupted. "Perhaps these two gentlemen will reflect and report anything that they recall—anything that might be of assistance?"

Castor and Pollux nodded vigorously, and Buckley surrendered in disgust. "I guess that'll have to do—for now." He looked around for other potential witnesses among the small group of spectators. "Hey, you! Professor—"

"Silva. Gilvie Silva." The academic responded with a worried look, glancing repeatedly at the occupant of the stretcher. "Detective—Buckley, is it? This is a dreadful thing. Such a young man, a brilliant mind. A terrible accident."

"You think so, do you?" Buckley snapped. "Anyway, how do you come to be here, so late in the day?"

"I was at the library for several hours after the evening meal, and my way home took me across campus, near enough to see that the police were here," Silva replied evenly. "Do you imply that I am a suspicious person, a-a suspect, Detective?"

Chan interjected.

"How could learned academic be suspected by police when he has just pronounced this death to be an accident?" Silva hesitated, his eyes darting back and forth between his two questioners.

"I apologize, I meant only . . . it is my English, my bad

English that makes my meaning unclear."

"Please allow me to disagree," Chan replied. "I also have added English tongue to my native language, and I think you speak well. And," he added, "your meaning is very clear."

Buckley scoffed. "Well, I will be wanting to have a few words with you, Professor, once we get things sorted out."

"I am free to go, then?"

"Sure, sure. Just don't go too far. My office will be in touch."

Silva offered a cross between a nod and a bow to the two men and walked rapidly away.

Buckley sighed.

"I just plain don't like the looks of that fellow. I don't know if he's a killer or not, but he's up to something."

"Guilty man sometimes act guilty. But innocent man sometimes act guilty, too." Chan grinned. "This Silva, maybe he is guilty of something. But what?"

The next morning's work was hardly underway in the Winterslip offices when Rose burst into John Winterslip's office unannounced.

"Well, to what do I owe this sudden visitation?" The young man rose from behind his cluttered desk, extinguishing a half-smoked cigarette in a marble ashtray.

"John, I think it's time." The young woman seated herself in front of the desk as Winterslip resumed his seat, pushing the ashtray to one side. "The investigation—"

"Have you heard something new from your father? He was here last evening—I was working late—"

"You're *always* working late," Rose replied, raising an eyebrow. "All work and no play . . . "

"I may be dull, but I am reliable," Winterslip

returned, spiritedly. "At least, Inspector Chan thinks so. As for the investigation," he said, "events seem to be moving rather rapidly. My humble efforts on the financial side of the puzzle are bearing fruit, but perhaps you haven't heard about last night's discovery?"

Rose shook her head. Winterslip explained briefly.

"The morning papers had only the barest mention of a body being found near the university, but your father no doubt has more information."

"I'll ask him. But have you told him everything?"

Winterslip frowned.

"My professional relationship with Inspector Chan has to come first right now, and he has far too much on his mind for me to muddy the waters further."

"And what about his trust in you—how can you keep anything secret from someone when . . .?" Her voice trailing off, the young woman's expression was equal parts anger and frustration.

Winterslip's face lengthened. Conflicting motives collided within him.

"Rose, I know you're worried," he said softly. "And I promise to do my best on all fronts.

"Secrets included."

Putting personal misgivings behind her, Rose left the Winterslip offices and headed for campus. She was looking forward to the two busiest days of the academic year—for her, anyway—since commencement would be held tomorrow, and preparations would be the focus of activity for today. A thousand minor points of logistical and ceremonial detail fell to the provost's office; she and Gertrude Winget shared responsibility for many of them. And, as the newest administrative support staff member, she often performed tasks Winget had tired of after many years of annual drudgery.

In the provost's office and elsewhere on campus, everyone's mind was not on commencement, however; conversations focused almost exclusively on the death of the chemistry professor Eduardo Dimayuga. Accident? Murder? Everyone had a theory, even though most had not known Dimayuga personally.

Rose was as curious as anyone, but duty called. She reported to Gertrude Winget in the auditorium, which had been festooned with ceremonial banners in preparation for the annual awarding of degrees, and the two went about their work. Today's rehearsal would allow those with ceremonial roles—the provost, president, dean, some faculty—to go through their paces, so that all would go off without a hitch at commencement tomorrow.

"If we can just get through tomorrow," Winget grumbled, "maybe things can begin to settle down a bit. People can't seem to concentrate on why we're all here—all they want to do is gossip and worry and speculate."

"Well, you have to admit—two people have died," Rose began, but Winget was having none of it.

"People die all the time," she snapped. "We haven't even heard definitely that either of these deaths was a murder. Trouble is, people like to create their own drama—and the faculty are no better than the students. Everybody"—she punctuated her words with the hammering of a tack into the edge of a sign, for emphasis—"wants to be Sherlock Holmes."

"There." Winget stepped back from her task, and picked up a leather folder from a nearby chair. "Now that things are in place for the rehearsal, please take this with you and keep it safe until tomorrow."

"What is it?" Rose accepted the folder, holding it gingerly.

"A commencement script, agenda, and general guide—all in one." Winget ticked off on her fingers the folder's main items. "The approved remarks of the provost, the order of the awarding of degrees—for the dean's benefit—and the approved remarks of the president. Don't let it out of your sight until you place it on the lectern tomorrow"—she pointed toward the center of the stage—"because the ceremony would be a disaster without it. We can't have several highly educated gentlemen awarding degrees willy-nilly. Or perhaps I should say, *ad libitum*."

Rose promised to keep the commencement manual-cum-scripture secure until the next day, and the two women watched as provost, dean, president and other participants refreshed their collective memory as to the proper way to conduct the hallowed academic ceremony.

All three men—Merriweather, Bernardo and Emerson—seemed unsettled, Rose observed. The provost, whose role would loom large at the start of the program, was impatient, even abrupt, in his verbal exchanges with others. Bernardo was, as usual, absentminded; but he seemed even more flustered than usual. The president's speaking role at commencement was confined to a valediction, one that would send graduates forth into the wide world, armed with academic degrees, yet he spoke sharply to both provost and dean, offering erroneous corrections. It was as if, Rose thought, his mind was elsewhere, and he was harboring some discontent that surfaced in his pointed comments.

"I hope they behave themselves better than this tomorrow," said Winget, under her breath.

You and me both, Rose thought.

CHAPTER XII

TANGLED SKEIN OF CLUES

Chan awoke early the next morning to the insistent ringing of the telephone. He cast aside the bedclothes and answered the call.

"Charlie? Buckley here. Sorry to disturb you so early, but this can't wait."

"Happy to hear latest news from colleague," Chan replied calmly.

"It's like I thought—somebody wanted to get that Dimayuga, maybe help him go for an unexpected swim. In all the confusion last night, I missed a message down at the station house. Seems our dead chemistry professor called me, left an urgent message, sometime not long before—"

"Message indicate nature of urgency?"

"No, not exactly, but it's like I told you before—the money business, then the library. Then the lady professor dies, then this Dimayuga calls me. Then he turns up dead. I think they're all related."

Chan imagined Buckley pausing to wipe a fevered brow.

"I have not come to identical conclusion, but you have made strong case. If all events are the work of one man, one person, then you have suspect in mind?"

Buckley sighed.

"That professor—Silva—he's my top choice. But what's his motive? After him," Buckley continued, "I have a long list of people who couldn't be guilty, or probably aren't."

"Many names on this list?" Chan inquired politely.

"Starting with the president, who was in Sacramento for meetings. The provost, who was with you from the library till the body was discovered. And the list goes on from there, with just about every single one of those"— frustration prompted Buckley's use of a few Anglo-Saxon expressions—"seeming to have an alibi that my men can't shake. Silva is the one exception. And he's made some strong statements about, well, stirring things up. Maybe with violence."

"You think he commits these acts himself or conspires with others?"

"All I know for sure is he's involved enough that taking him to the station house is my best bet," Buckley retorted. "And I want to send a message to whoever's involved that we're on to them. Arresting him and spreading the word will do that, and I think some private conversation with the esteemed Professor Silva will get us a lot farther along than we've gotten so far. But what about you? I know you said we'd compare notes later, but have you found anything that rules Silva out?"

"Cannot say that Silva is innocent as newly arrived infant," Chan admitted. "Only ask one favor of you before we compare notes, and that is—"

"Yeah?"

"That you wait until this afternoon, and arrest Silva in public setting on university campus. This will 'send message,' as you say, and several hours' delay will give me time to gather last threads and untangle all those I have gathered. Each thread is part of answer, but together they

TANGLED SKEIN OF CLUES 121

are currently snarled in a knot."

"And you think a few hours will make a real difference?" Buckley demanded.

"I cannot guarantee success, but in keeping with old Chinese saying, my study has started at the bottom and worked its way upward—like pole climber. To reveal truth and aid your investigation—those are my goals."

Having convinced Buckley to postpone the arrest, Chan concluded the call and reflected for a moment. His unofficial methods had indeed resulted in a tangled skein of clues, and he was confident that the truth could be revealed. But he needed one more unassailable fact. By itself, it would mean nothing in a court of law. But as a means to an end . . .

His notebook yielded John Quincy's home telephone number. His investigative protégé answered promptly.

"Charlie! You're up and about early this morning—"

"Pardon my intrusion on your household," Chan interrupted. "Rudeness seems to be new habit for me. I have urgent need for driver of fast car to act as my chauffeur today."

"Then I'm your man—just give me 30 minutes to collect myself, and I'll be at your doorstep. You can fill me in then."

The connection was severed by both men simultaneously. Chan made two more calls, then prepared to meet his driver.

Commencement at the university was both a solemn occasion and a celebration; an end—to years of study, for the prospective graduates—and (as its name indicates) a beginning: the start of, in theory, long and successful lives made possible by higher education's formal transmission of knowledge. The ceremonial trappings—all participants in academic regalia, the banners, music, the formal procession—tended to put nervous souls on edge, even in a normal year.

Clearly, this was not a normal year.

Recent events would have been on most participants' minds even without a noticeable police presence in the back of the auditorium. Detective Buckley and the redoubtable Officer Mallory were accompanied by two uniformed officers, and the small but doughty law enforcement contingent was trying—unsuccessfully—to make itself inconspicuous. The number of participants and attendees filled the venue to its capacity, and beyond. Late arrivals stood in back, behind the last row of fixed seats, craning to see the pomp and circumstance.

Rose had arrived early, installing the all-important leather folder at the lectern and taking her place in the wings. She had no public role in the ceremony, but needed to be close at hand in case some last-minute task needed to be tackled. From her vantage point she could see all of the stage and much of the auditorium's frontmost seating. Like many present, she had other matters on her mind— especially a truly odd job that she had performed as the result of her father's early morning phone call. Gertrude Winget was also in the wings, on the opposite side. They exchanged a wave and waited for the procession to begin.

Suddenly, the pre-commencement mood was shattered as the police quartet advanced on Gilvie Silva, who had taken his place with other faculty near the tail end of the procession.

"Come along, Professor," Buckley grunted. "You don't want to make a big scene in front of all these

TANGLED SKEIN OF CLUES 123

nice people, do you?"

Silva sneered inarticulately, but went quietly with the police contingent, out of the auditorium. Word of his arrest spread through the ranks of professors and other commencement participants, all the way to the highest ranks, in seconds.

"Whatever Dad has in mind," Rose thought, "I hope it happens—and that he gets here in time to see it."

As the car sped around a curve Chan held onto his hat, more of a reflex action than a necessity. The sedan's windows were closed, and there was no possibility that anything would fly from the vehicle. And John Winterslip was an excellent driver, a necessity given the urgency of the detective's errand and the need for his presence at commencement.

"What I'm not understanding, Charlie," Winterslip said, loudly enough to be heard over the auto's thrumming horsepower, "is the need for this mad dash with yours truly. Don't mistake me; I enjoy a speedy tour of the California countryside as much as anyone. But I'm curious—"

Chan grinned and interrupted his willing chauffeur. "Remember doomed feline whose unhappy fate resulted from inquisitive nature, and be patient. All will be made clear in time."

"You're the detective-in-charge," Winterslip returned with a laugh, downshifting to avoid a collision with a delivery truck. "I'm the amateur assistant sleuth. And Grand Prix contestant," he concluded, as their sedan passed the truck and accelerated toward the university, still some miles distant.

The ceremony began shortly after Silva's arrest, on time

and without additional incident, and the order of business proceeded. The provost offered the standard welcome and accompanying remarks concerning academic achievement, the ceremony, the celebratory nature of the day; and candidates for degrees crossed the stage, one by one, to receive diplomas. Rose watched the scene with a growing sense of unease.

Where was Charlie Chan? His specific instructions to her had been followed, and he had assured her that he would be present; but there was no sign of him. Peering from her position in the wings toward the back of the hall, Rose began to fear the worst.

"Daughter's view of ceremony sufficient?"

"Dad!"

Rose turned, embracing a grinning Charlie Chan, as Gertrude Winget raised a stern forefinger to her lips. The two Chans retreated a few steps from the curtain's edge, continuing their reunion in whispers.

"Where have you been? I was worried!"

"Concern from favored daughter most gratifying," Chan said, with one eye on events unfolding on the stage nearby. "I have engaged in last-minute fact checking, accompanied by speedy driver John Winterslip.

"But," he continued, "all seems to be well here. Ceremony is near to conclusion?" Rose nodded. "And you have performed small favor for parent?" His expression was serious. "Pages you inserted into presidential script very important to what now may follow, and much may be revealed as a result."

"Sure, all set," Rose said, without pause. "Just like you told me, but I don't see—"

"Hush!" Chan warned. "President is about to speak."

The diplomas had, indeed, been awarded, and the

TANGLED SKEIN OF CLUES   125

newly minted university graduates had returned to their seats. Christopher Emerson took his place at the lectern, smiled at the assemblage, and began to read the scripted valediction from the pages within the leather folder that Rose had guarded so well.

"As president of the university, I take great pride in offering you this valedictory message as we conclude a great and wonderful occasion," Emerson proclaimed in a somewhat theatrical voice, his idea of what the leader of a great institution should sound like. His tendency toward declamation failed to grab the weary audience's full attention. Like all such ceremonies, the commencement program had already been quite long—and an unscheduled police action had not contributed to its charm. As the first page of his script gave way to a second, and a third, signs and sounds of polite impatience arose.

"In conclusion," Emerson boomed, as he turned to the fourth page of his remarks. Some in the auditorium sighed with relief. "Let us take a moment to honor the two members of our university community who could not be with us today—" he paused, turning to the previous page briefly before continuing—"due to their untimely passing."

A slight frown creased the presidential brow.

"Eduardo Dimayuga was a brilliant chemist, scholar, researcher, teacher and colleague. We feel his loss keenly, but his legacy goes forth into the world today, as it has for some years, in the persons of those he taught. The result of his work here, a profound impact on their lives, will continue."

Clearing his throat, Emerson paused while turning yet another page—Dimayuga's brief moment of remembrance had apparently occupied a page all its own—and continued.

"Our other colleague whose recent departure from life we mourn, Milly—Mildred Stark, a member of our university . . . family for many years—"

The president seemed to be reading the script with difficulty; his voice no longer carried to the back of the auditorium.

"In tribute to her memory, these words—" his face paled—"these words best evoke her spirit:

> '*Guess now who holds thee?*' –
> '*Death,*' *I said, But, there,*
> *The silver answer rang,* –"

Emerson's voice fell silent. His eyes closed and head bowed; as the silence lengthened, even the least attentive graduates realized that some unscripted moment, some personal struggle, was playing out.

The president mastered himself, departed from whatever remained of his valedictory message and recited the closing declaration of the ceremony, the words tumbling out in a rush:

"I declare this annual commencement ceremony of the university to be concluded."

Closing the folder hastily, he turned and walked into the wings, where Chan and Rose waited. The provost and dean followed in the president's wake, and Winget crossed the stage to join them.

"Please," Chan said to the group. "We have matters to discuss not suitable for this public place." Some graduates lingered in the auditorium, looking toward the stage to see what was happening.

The provost took charge, leading the way to the room where they had donned caps and gowns before the ceremony. They were greeted by a decidedly non-academic voice.

"Well, well, well. All graduated, are we?" Buckley's light tone belied his grim expression. He and Mallory stood on either side of a disgruntled Silva, still clad in his ceremonial gown, tasseled cap in hand. Wooden folding chairs enough for the new arrivals were arranged in a semicircle, as though for a small-group class discussion.

"I must apologize to my colleagues for ending the ceremony so abruptly," Emerson began, as they took seats in response to Buckley's direction. "I don't know what came over me—"

"Don't you, Christopher?" The provost glared at Emerson. "You, of all people—"

"Please!" Chan held up a restraining hand. "Maintain dignity attached to academic profession, and permit me to make remarks of interest to all here. With kind permission of proper authorities?" He turned to Buckley, who nodded. Chan continued:

"Problems at this place, like Chinese bittersweet vine, start small and grow over time. My invitation here, not known to all of you, was to make investigation of college finances"—some of the academics stirred in their seats—"with daughter's presence providing excuse for visit. With help of experts, evidence was uncovered pointing to some manipulation of college accounts."

"Outrageous!" Provost Merriweather fumed, half-rising from his chair. "Do you mean to insinuate—"

"Please to remain seated," Chan interjected. "No insinuation. Only facts, all of which will be turned over to police and district attorney."

"But then," he continued, "bigger events overtake small investigation. First, library explosion, fire. Body of unfortunate Professor Stark found on same day. Police look for connection between all these. And they are right," he nodded to Buckley, "connected, but not to same person. Evil events are like different branches of bittersweet vine.

"In the case of money," Chan went on, "sums involved not large enough to overturn workings of university, but big enough to create possible scandal when discovered. Perpetrator acted not for gain, but to cause disruption. Angry professor often spoke of upsetting established order—could have wanted to blacken reputation of noble institution." Eyes turned toward Silva, who smiled at Chan.

"This, what you say, these things—lies," he returned. "I have no interest in university money, no time for trivial matters."

"But time for making louder disturbance, knowledge of same," Chan said calmly. "You were part of conversation, not actor, but maybe willing to remain silent, as chemistry colleague devised clever explosive device to cause panic in library."

Exclamations tumbled from the group, as Silva loudly denied involvement.

"You did not act," Chan repeated, "but you knew enough to prevent dangerous demonstration, and did nothing to prevent it. Police experts determined that knowledge of chemistry was necessary to construct bomb that could have killed. You hoped that effort undertaken by deceased professor, your friend Dimayuga, would cause great disturbance, not for personal gain, but to make political statement about world affairs."

Buckley could contain himself no longer.

"So we were right all along," he declared. "Lost your nerve after your big talk blew up and caught fire, and you got scared. Maybe your bomb-making friend would turn

TANGLED SKEIN OF CLUES   129

on you, and you didn't like the idea of prison so you invited him to go swimming?"

"No!" Silva shouted. "Not me! He told me—he said someone wanted to make trouble for the university, to upset the administration. Bring dishonor. They had promised him—"

"Promotion, perhaps? Opportunities for career that only the highest official in the university can bring about?" Chan turned toward a subdued President Emerson.

"No, Inspector Chan," the president replied, his expression a mix of sadness and resignation. "Not I. But I am beginning to understand what you're driving at."

"Only one person had motive for these things—to build atmosphere of failure by creating money troubles and violence, so institution's trustees would lose confidence in leader of university. Plan would have made way for one who desires power over others, person stifled by years spent waiting for opportunity—"

"Gordon!" Winget gasped.

"You"—Chan looked directly at the provost—"are murderer. You killed chemistry professor who threatened to reveal that you were architect of these events."

"Damn you," Merriweather fumed through gritted teeth, "and damn him—he threatened me with blackmail if I didn't advance his research funding and promotion. I would've been tied to him for life."

Buckley advanced on the provost with handcuffs. "Gordon Merriweather, you're under arrest for the murders of—"

"Wait, no!" Merriweather shouted. "Only Dimayuga— I had nothing to do with that woman's death."

Chan nodded. "Even one who has done evil can still speak the truth. You did not kill Mildred Stark."

Dean Bernardo, bewildered by the avalanche of disclosures, roused himself, exclaiming: "Then, by the Lord Harry, who did?"

"Not you," Chan replied, "even though you concealed discovery of body. Unsuspecting woman"—he nodded toward Winget—"entered room not long after you left, finding what you had already seen."

Bernardo's eyes widened beneath bushy brows. "But how did you—"

"You made unscheduled visit to room, made terrible discovery and, perhaps thinking victim still lived, wiped blood from her face. Realizing that she was dead, you made hasty departure from room, leaving it unlocked, and arrived in much-disturbed state at meeting where library event was under discussion," Chan recounted. "Yet you spoke of multiple unfortunate events—as though referring to something not known to those in room. Later, you excused self for private examination of hands, to ensure traces of blood had been removed."

The dean was downcast. "I'm ashamed to admit it, everything you say is true, Mr. Chan. I have a horror of violence, and my reaction was unworthy. I'm prepared to submit to the authorities for my failure to act, for my attempt to distance myself from this terrible event."

"Authorities may look upon actions as less than criminal, especially compared to those of the one who was in the room before your visit there. Very few minutes ago," Chan continued, "President Emerson made speech, shorter than expected, I think. And he did not complete poetic words in script intended to honor memory of dead woman." He pulled a small book from his pocket and opened it. "Maybe I can finish what he started?"

'Guess now who holds thee?' –
'Death,' I said, But, there,
The silver answer rang, –
'Not Death, but Love,'

"Not Death, but Love," Chan repeated. "You knew this lady long ago, and there was great affection between you. But something else, I think. And she confronted you—here, in this room—and died."

Emerson's ashen face turned toward Chan, eyes brimming with tears.

"You're right, Mr. Chan. But I didn't kill her. She was—unsettled, perhaps unhinged. Asked to meet me, secretly—even suggested the place and time, when I was supposed to be in Sacramento. She was distraught, confronted me with our shared past. Thrust that book"—he gestured toward the *Sonnets* in Chan's hand—"at me, stumbled and fell into the mace. I could see that she was dead, and I panicked. After all this time, I thought, everything I had worked for would be gone. I was a coward, and I ran away—but it was an accident."

"Not for us to decide," Chan remarked. "You will have opportunity to convince others—prosecutor, judge, jury."

Buckley and Mallory took charge of the two men, exiting the ill-fated room. Silva approached Chan, extending a hand.

"I want to thank you, Inspector, for arranging matters. And congratulate you for your success."

Chan nodded.

"Maybe academic, freed from legal complications by cooperation, will now return to more peaceful pursuits—in classroom?"

Silva hesitated. "Maybe," he admitted. "But I am not

sure what the future holds for me. And the world grows more troubled."

"You, I think, want to play a more active role in international matters," Chan noted. "But remember ancient saying: 'The farther one travels, the less one knows.' Maybe knowledge-seeking professor will go far—but truth remain elusive?"

Silva smiled and took his leave.

CHAPTER XIII
ONE LAST MYSTERY SOLVED

"But you haven't explained nearly enough," Rose protested.

The two Chans and John Winterslip were breakfasting in Chan's hotel restaurant. It was the detective's last morning on the mainland, and all preparations for his passage home had been completed. The university was just starting to come to terms with its abrupt change in leadership, and a nine days' wonder of newspaper coverage was underway. The university trustees had met in emergency session, approving a reluctant Dean Bernardo to serve as acting president for the time being. The former president and former provost were jailed while their expensive attorneys scrambled to arrange bail, if they could find a judge to allow it.

"The lady has a point," Winterslip agreed. "What led you away from Silva? The police seemed to think he was their man."

Chan grinned. "Noisy professor was always on edge of events, like dog that herds flock—running back and forth, snapping, but not biting the sheep. Not entirely innocent, legally."

He turned to Rose.

"It was Professor Silva who arranged with waitress to deliver note when we enjoyed tea at Locus Bonum. Please consider," Chan continued, "that note did not threaten violence, and made vague reference to 'justice.' Same call to improve society, fix international troubles that this Silva had made in hearing of others.

"But trail of clues to real author of these events started with financial investigation," he continued. "Who would go to such trouble for so little money? Who had access to records? Long-time secretary had no motive, and president had nothing to gain from creating scandal that would bring shame to his leadership. Venerable dean? But it was his effort to probe unsettling situation that prompted investigation.

"Provost, though, had much to gain. Impression of him suggested one who would lead, if he could; one whose goal was higher than present station. Conversations with others—and examination of his professional history—also pointed to a would-be president.

"Outside library, when many were present, provost and angry professor Silva both appeared to humble self to possess some guilty knowledge." He grinned. "All Chan offspring have heard ancient parent proclaim that Chinese—"

"—are psychic people," Rose finished. "And that's what led you to the provost?"

"More accurate to say that it was some part of solution," Chan replied. "Each piece of jigsaw puzzle needed to complete whole picture."

Breakfast was over. Winterslip lit a cigarette, raising it to pose a question.

"Our little trip to and from Sacramento—what was that all about?"

"Point did not arise when former president admitted confrontation with lady professor," Chan said, "but maybe it will be significant if case goes to trial. President always stayed at same place in Sacramento when traveling on university business. Not on campus when body was found, he said, because duty required his presence at state capital for two days while staying two nights at Hotel Senator.

"Thanks to speedy driver, examination of hotel registry revealed president stayed only one night in capital city. Why did he insist on two nights, lying about time of return to campus? Because he wished to conceal meeting with unfortunate professor.

"Also, academic persons leave trail of diplomas, places of study, and such was the case with this Emerson. Small amount of time in public library revealed that his past absence from this city, to study in Philadelphia, happened when younger version of Mildred Stark was also present in that city—and at same university."

Chan paused, taking a sip of tea.

"Coincidence? Did they know each other then, so many years ago? Book of love poems under body pointed to some romantic history. But how to connect deceased woman here with long-ago relationship in different place? Career history of each included time in Philadelphia, at same institution, prompting further attention to that possibility.

"Fortune smiled on my efforts," Chan continued, thinking of June Kirk. "Attorney friend made inquiries through proper channels, and discovered marriage license filing for Christopher Robert Emerson and Mildred Stanhope Stark, languishing in Philadelphia recorder of deeds files.

"So, they were married?" Rose exclaimed.

"Not likely," her father replied. "Search of Philadelphia newspaper records from that time reveal only brief announcement of engagement, but no news of wedding. Whether relationship ended before wedding could happen, or brief marriage failed in some way—who can say? But engagement announcement spoke of proposed groom's social status, while prospective bride's family was described in humbler words—perhaps this posed obstacle for ambitious young man."

"Maybe he broke it off after his parents kicked up a fuss, or maybe he just couldn't go through with it," Winterslip mused. "Already had lofty notions and didn't want to be tied to an inconvenient spouse."

"'Where there is education, there is no distinction of class,'" Chan quoted. "Maybe ancient philosopher was wrong in this case."

"But why the meeting between them, after so many years?" Rose looked puzzled. "She had been at the university for a few years. Why didn't she have it out with him before?"

"Autopsy show unfortunate woman suffered from terminal affliction of brain," Chan said solemnly. "Were her actions guided by diseased intellect, as president claims? Or a lifetime's regret for lost love? Her time was short, and she sought to confront the past. And the man who long ago abandoned her."

Rose sighed. "I guess that clears everything up."

"Not so fast!" Winterslip piped up. "How did the goings-on at the library connect up to all this?"

"Thought you would never ask." Chan grinned. "You have heard, maybe, ancient Roman proverb that credit for victory is owned by all, but blame for defeat goes unclaimed? Responsibility for library bomb shared by provost, who wanted incident to disrupt institution—bringing discredit to university president, and faculty. Provost knew outspoken scholar would embrace tactic that caused disturbance, and this Silva enlisted like-minded colleague,

ONE LAST MYSTERY SOLVED   137

Dimayuga, who possessed knowledge to create weapon of war.

"Very fortunate," Chan continued soberly, "that no lives were lost in explosion and smoky fire. Reckless men were prepared to cause multiple deaths to achieve their goals."

Rose and Winterslip fell silent for a moment. Rose started—an unresolved element had occurred to her.

"Castor and Pollux! What about them?"

Charlie Chan grinned. "Gossipy old men with know-it-all reputation were, please pardon the expression, all smoke and no fire. From library to money to untimely deaths—all these events seem to have happened without their knowledge, direct or indirect."

Rose was unconvinced. "But-but they always turn up, and everyone says—"

"What everyone believes certain, no one knows for sure," Chan opined. "Frequently true that assumptions made by many turn out to be lacking in substance. Such was the case here."

"Now," the detective concluded. "One more mystery remains to be solved, and I have solution."

"Really? I think you covered everything," the younger man said. Clearing his throat, he continued earnestly. "But there is one more question we'd like to discuss with you—"

"I refer to mystery of wedding date and place," Chan's smile broadened. "San Francisco—or Honolulu?"

"Dad! How long have you known?" Rose said with a laugh.

"First indication occurred at dock when young man pretends he is not already well acquainted with daughter. Second, he who wishes to keep secret should avoid displaying photograph of loved one in office—where I spied same when visiting.

"And third clue," he reached out for Rose's hand, pointing to the fourth finger, "was indication of lighter-colored skin where engagement ring recently reposed. Temporarily removed, no doubt," he patted the hand affectionately, "so that it would not reveal plans before ritual conversation with father of intended bride."

The couple laughed.

"I guess we should've known better," Winterslip said happily, "than to try to outwit Charlie Chan."

CHAPTER XIV
NO GREATER CALAMITY

Charlie Chan was glad to be home; there was no substitute for the life of wife and family he enjoyed in the house on Punchbowl Hill.

Weeks had passed since his departure from San Francisco, and his normal investigative duties were something of a relief from the puzzle that had confronted him on the mainland. For the moment, the yearning for greater challenges was gone.

Rose's frequent letters kept him apprised of the university's recovery from crime and scandal; the academic community was resilient, and the institution would go on. The criminal courts had begun the lengthy process of sorting out the fates of Emerson and Merriweather, and former dean—now interim president—Bernardo was looking forward to a full retirement, once his successor was in place.

Chan laid aside Rose's most recent letter, and picked up the international postal card that had also arrived in today's mail.

Greetings Señor Chan,

I write these lines in haste to say that your faith in me has been justified. You made possible my agreement with the police—without your help I would be in American jail. Instead I do what must be done, to fight for my country. ¡No pasarán!

¡Viva la Republica!

Silva

Chan held the card for a moment, thinking of far-off struggles between nations, and the young men eager to take part in them. He murmured to himself the ancient philosopher's words:

There is no greater calamity than lightly engaging in war.

The detective looked out at the winking lights of Honolulu, lost in thought.

THE END

ACKNOWLEDGEMENTS

Above all, I am indebted to Earl Derr Biggers for creating the character of Charlie Chan; and to the real-life inspiration for Chan, Chang Apana. I also want to thank those who have encouraged this modest effort aimed at recapturing something of the original Chan novels: my spouse, Patricia Swann, to whom this book is dedicated; daughter Sarah Marris-Swann, whose artistry graces the cover designed by our friend, the talented and energetic Lynne Browne; my brother Bruce Swann, for his careful review and thoughtful suggestions; and publisher, partner and friend, Nick Burns, whose experience and expertise were invaluable.

ABOUT THE AUTHOR

John L. Swann has worked as a broadcast journalist, both in radio and television, and in public relations and marketing. His communications career has included stints as news director and anchor at WUTR-TV and anchor, reporter and talk show host at WIBX radio. After leaving broadcasting, he served as chief of staff to the president of the State University of New York Institute of Technology and authored *From the Mills to Marcy*, a history of the college. His work has been recognized by the Associated Press and the New York State Broadcasters Association, and he holds degrees in communication and information design and technology.

A native of the Midwest (he grew up on a farm and could still milk a cow if the occasion arises), Swann lives in Utica, New York, with his wife, Patricia, whose years of encouragement resulted in the publication of *Death, I Said*, his first work of fiction and the first in a series of Charlie Chan mysteries that will coincide with the approaching centennial of the character's 1925 debut.

Printed in the USA
CPSIA information can be obtained
at www.ICGtesting.com
CBHW021015191223
2698CB00001B/8